BACK ROADS

Also by Andrée A. Michaud
(in translation)

Boundary (The Last Summer)
The River of Dead Trees

BACK ROADS

ANDRÉE A. MICHAUD

TRANSLATED BY J. C. SUTCLIFFE

ARACHNIDE

First published as *Routes secondaires* in 2017 by Éditions Québec Amérique
First published in English in 2020 by House of Anansi Press Inc.
www.houseofanansi.com

24 23 22 21 20   1 2 3 4 5

Library and Archives Canada Cataloguing in Publication
Title: Back roads / Andrée A. Michaud ; translated by Juliet Sutcliffe.
Other titles: Routes secondaires. English
Names: Michaud, Andrée A., 1957– author. | Sutcliffe, J. C., translator.
Description: Translation of: Routes secondaires.
Identifiers: Canadiana (print) 20190165421 | Canadiana (ebook) 20190165456 | ISBN 9781487005801 (softcover) | ISBN 9781487005818 (EPUB) | ISBN 9781487005825 (Kindle)
Classification: LCC PS8576.I217 R6813 2020 | DDC C843/.54—dc23

Cover and text design: Alysia Shewchuk

 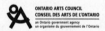

We acknowledge the financial support of the Government of Canada through the National Translation Program for Book Publishing, an initiative of the Action Plan for Official Languages —2018–2023: Investing in Our Future, *for our translation activities.*

Printed and bound in Canada

To P., for P. M.

All the characters in this novel lived between March 1, 2014, and January 19, 2017.

Then I went back into the house and wrote,
It is midnight. The rain is beating on the windows.
It was not midnight. It was not raining.
—Samuel Beckett, *Molloy*

I must be called Heather. She must be called Heather. I've been repeating these sentences over and over for months without managing to figure out what they mean. Little by little, they've lost their clarity and become an obsession.

I must be called Heather. She must be called Heather.

Fall was nearly over when these few words showed up and imposed themselves on me like an injunction, like some kind of obligation I'd be skeptical about if I were able to think more calmly. I was walking on the gravel road I'd known since childhood, keeping an eye out for furtive movements in the undergrowth, a rustling of leaves or a cracking of branches that would indicate the presence of an animal other than myself in the shifting shadows. With all my senses alert, I was imagining a novel in which I would convey the mysterious power of this undergrowth when suddenly I stopped right in the middle of the road, dumbstruck, murmuring, "I must be called Heather, she must be called Heather."

For a few moments, I was nothing more than these two interchangeable sentences, I must be called Heather, she must be called Heather, as if some truth buried under the weight of years had resurfaced in the sweet October wind.

I

And then I felt something bubbling up in me, the sort of relief that follows a long period of waiting, and I was finally able to relax. I had just sketched out the beginning of the novel I'd been seeking in the undergrowth.

I don't know how long I stood there, but the sun was setting when the noise of a car coming over the hill behind me forced me to step back toward the ditch, where soggy leaves lined the thin trail of a stream that widened out a little further on.

The car slowed down when it reached me, the woman driving it probably curious as to why I wasn't moving and suspecting some problem, a situation demanding that she stop and help me there and then, by the rapidly darkening forest. When our eyes met, I tried to convey the smile I felt blooming in me, as a feeling of peace filled me at last. But my smile quickly vanished when I realized the eyes looking back at me were my own.

Stunned by the resemblance, I retreated another step and raised my arms, as if to touch the face I was backing away from — the face of the woman scrutinizing me with widened eyes that were blue, just like mine — wanting to feel its features the way blind people do. And then, seeing her panic-stricken expression — the clichéd image that sprang to mind was of a doe being chased by a pack of wolves — I lowered my arms and signalled to her to carry on, that everything was fine. When her car disappeared around the bend, I went down to the stream, my quaking legs crumpling to the earth, to try to see my reflection in it. Kneeling down at the edge of the water, the trickle of which was too thin to reflect anything more than my fear, I dipped into the surface of the water with my fingertips and murmured a name, *Heather*, because I had understood, when our incredulous eyes recognized each other, that the woman in the car was called Heather, that she had to be called Heather, and that henceforth our fates would be inextricably linked.

I.

Sometimes circumstances conspire to change a life forever. The banality of this statement, as unoriginal as the image I'd entertained of a panic-stricken deer, only renders it more true, especially when you have been feeling no desire whatsoever to change the course of events, nor yearning for an accident or a miracle to turn your world upside down. Expecting nothing, you merely postpone a meeting, stare at the sky—weather's not good—and jump into your car, planning to take shelter in a movie theatre while rain pours down over the city. And then the bad weather catches up with you and you never make it to the theatre to see that movie you weren't much interested in seeing anyway, a thriller you'd only selected for the pleasure of admiring the sweat-glistening muscles of its celebrity actor.

That's what happened that day. I went to the movies.

My work was going nowhere. I was moving around in circles and couldn't summon up any interest in the words lined up in front of me, my thoughts constantly drifting off to the blue sky and the clouds. Instead of concentrating on the page I'd scrawled over too much, or helping P. to repair the fence demarcating a section of our property,

I'd jumped into my car, true to the woman wanting to be secluded in the darkness of a cinema with Brad Pitt, Bruce Willis, or Clive Owen, and headed for the 4th Line, where I parked in an empty spot near the first bend in the road, the point beyond which my gaze would meet Heather's.

Would I have noticed Heather had I arrived ten minutes earlier or later, if I'd decided to go and buy the papers before my walk or go say hi to an old friend? And if I had seen her then, would the meeting have had the same significance, the same consequences?

Ever since that day in October when I left the house anticipating nothing, I've wondered what would have happened if I'd put down the work that was boring me sooner, or if for instance I'd walked somewhere else along the road people around here call La Languette, after the part of the forest it dissects. It's a route I'd likely walked every Sunday afternoon of the previous winter, looking for shadows in the undergrowth, listening for dry branches cracking, imagining an armed man leaping out of the bleak woods, someone who, not hesitating to shoot, would reduce me to being the victim of a tragic hunting accident, one of those characters you come across in novels only because they actually exist in real life.

Perhaps it was fear of this man, whose violence was more in keeping with fall, that inspired me to turn left at the entrance to the village and hurry toward another destiny — toward, who knows, my own violent nature. Because I don't yet know where that decision will lead me, the one I took on that October afternoon when time weighed so heavily on me, impelling me to get in my car, turn left, park by the first bend on the 4th Line, and leave my vehicle in order to feel the earth beneath my feet, stopping in front of the undergrowth behind which rises a mound where blueberries grow so abundantly every August.

I don't yet know because the story has hardly begun and will inevitably be subject to a chain of events to which I'll have to defer, for the simple reason that being suspicious of even the slightest sunny spell, of the most insignificant of unexpected visits, runs the risk of your no longer being able to tell true from false. All I can do is anticipate the events that will, from now on, determine the fate of a woman named Heather, in other words, my own fate, because I know without a shadow of a doubt the story won't stop there: the machine is already in motion, and any attempts I make to stop its momentum will do nothing but trigger repercussions—and, I fear, incidents as unpredictable as they are disastrous.

I never again saw Heather at the wheel of her car, an old-model Buick that churned up thick, stagnant clouds of dust in the dense air. Every afternoon for two weeks, I went back to the same gravel road at sunset, ready to wave in a gesture of recognition as soon as the Buick appeared over the hill. But Heather never came that way again, never at that hour when the woods dissolve into shadow, cleaving the world into two opposed universes: one in which cars drive toward the setting sun, still free for a time, and another in which they recede into the forest.

By the end of the fifteenth afternoon, knowing that I would never again see Heather fleeing in the dusky light, I decided it was time to wrestle with the destiny of a woman who, simply by the fact of her existence, had encroached on my own.

I went back home, double-locked my study door and then, sitting in front of a brand-new notebook, placed Heather's car across the road leading to a cabin by the first bend of the 4th Line. After hesitating for a few seconds, I closed my eyes in order to conjure up Heather's panic-stricken smile, the image of the doe, my pen gliding over the bright white paper. The Buick appeared, and I pressed down on the gas pedal.

A radio was crackling inside the car, and a young woman was announcing glorious weather for the following day. That's the actual word she used, *glorious*, just like the sun, its last rays hitting Heather's rear-view mirror and blinding her. This was also the last word Heather heard, *glorious*, perhaps even the last word she murmured, surrounded as she was by the beauty of the setting sun before the trees leaned aside to make space for her car as it skidded in a shower of chromatic sparks; before the branches of balsam pines shattered the windshield as the engine groaned and a squeal of metal announced she'd arrived at her destination, a place from which she could neither move forward nor retreat, in the heart of darkness.

I've been trying to sleep for two hours now, but every time I'm about to drop off, I'm yanked unceremoniously from slumber by noises of crumpling metal mingled with Heather's voice reminding me it's going to be a beautiful day tomorrow. *Glorious*, she gasps, *glorious* . . .

In the darkness I see my alarm clock's phosphorescent numbers and wonder about the motives that compelled me to bring Heather back, pressing hard on the gas pedal, abandoning her in the woods, and forcing her to set off on a hike whose destination I do not know.

The more the night wears on, the more my insomnia-induced anxiety makes me question whether I've made the right choices. By the weak light of my alarm clock, the certainty contained within the two phrases, "I must be called Heather, she must be called Heather," no longer seems as clear as it had at the end of the afternoon when they had, by virtue of their suddenness, seemed as clear as the eye of the cat watching me from the foot of the bed. What had at first seemed an imperative — my name must be Heather, I have no choice but to be called Heather — slowly dissolved in the verb's imprecision and became nothing more than one possibility among many: I *must be* Heather, I *think* I'm Heather, I'm *probably* Heather.

I turn these possibilities over and over without managing to conclude anything concrete, because none of the options throws light upon the nature of my relationship with the woman whose name was revealed to me just before fate arranged our encounter. The meeting to which we were both invited ought to have been enough to convince me, but the night draws me into thoughts that aren't exactly conducive to the reconciliation which needs to happen between Heather and me if I'm not to remain permanently stuck in the mire of that fall day when I decided to set out on the 4th Line.

For the hundredth time, I recall the colour of the sky when I got out of the car, the yellowish light of the birches contrasting with the shadows accumulating beneath the pines, the barely audible rustling of the branches, and then the silence that had enveloped me when, in the middle of the dusty road, I'd murmured, "I must be called Heather." For the hundredth time, I softly repeat the decree that haunts me, "I must, I must . . ." and calmness finally joins the silence.

I'm not mistaken. I really am called Heather. Heather Thorne. She's called Heather Thorne.

It was completely dark when Heather Thorne emerged from the limbo she'd been thrown into by the impact. In front of her, the clock glowing on the dashboard — the only element linking her with the world she's come from — shows quarter after midnight, but she doesn't understand what those numbers mean any more than she understands the blood smearing the windshield. Temporarily, Heather Thorne has lost her memory. She is, temporarily, a purely mechanical object; she owes the meagre consciousness animating the surface of her gaze, as she stares out into the night, to the blood beating in her veins.

As for my own gaze into the darkness, it's one of feebleness. Falling stars cast vague patterns on the curtains blowing in the wind, and, with the cat beside me, I sink into peaceful sleep as, far away, the sound of screeching metal that has been drowning out the cries of blackbirds abates.

It's quarter after seven when the smell of coffee pulls me out of the forest where Heather, stuck inside her car, watches the glowing clock of my insomniac night. Feeling serene, I go downstairs to join P., who is busy at the kitchen counter. I kiss his neck and say, "Good morning, my darling." I pour myself a cup of coffee and, after consuming three slices of bread and cream cheese, go outside to see the sun. Truly, the day will be glorious.

A silk moth or hawk moth — I'm not very good on moths, but it's some kind of bombyx — keeps banging into the lamp lighting my desk. It's quarter after midnight and I've just written the sentence "Why 'Heather'?"

I read it again: "Why 'Heather'?"

From his armchair, the cat keeps an eye on the bombyx, which is now trapped in the lampshade, crashing into it with a desperate fluttering of its wings, or at least that's how I interpret its agitation. It's the survival instinct kicking in, a manifestation of despair. With its wings spread, the little creature hits the lampshade with a strength that pushes living things far away from everything that could pose a danger to it, until a desire more powerful than its fragile will to stay alive makes it come back and throw itself at the bulb. I convince myself I can almost hear the noise of its feet sizzling.

Why Heather?

It's because of the name's sonority, the warmth I

ascribe to it—*heat, to heat, to heat up*—when really it should evoke a landscape. *Heath.* Moorland covered in a purple flowering shrub. The flames licking at the name that appeared before me in the October chill are merely an illusion, I know, but I like maintaining this illusion, imagining a spark setting fire to the heather while the roaring blaze smothers the sound of someone yelling my original first name—Andrée, a name whose ambivalence designates me both male and female, an androgynous person whose femininity hangs on a silent vowel.

It's Heather's deceptive warmth that has seduced me, like the light luring in the moth that has just smashed into my desk, its legs beating at the air with a mildly convulsive movement. In the morning, I will find it dead in the same spot.

I can hear P. snoring behind the dividing wall, P., who is unaware he is no longer simply my partner, but also that of a woman named Heather Thorne. I'm not telling him. He'll realize soon enough, when, with shards of glass hanging from her wet hair, Heather comes back from the tiny clearing where her car stopped—if she ever does come back—and he'll see her talking to me, two identical women sitting face to face at my desk, where, remonstrating at the heavens, they'll determine their futures.

Tonight the sky is clear and I can't sleep. I count the cracks in the ceiling and wonder if my intervention could have saved the bombyx and if it is still possible to save Heather from a night of pain and fear. Of course, I could always rip out the page in which I determine that her Buick will be driven into the forest and instead let it fly toward the setting sun, but in order to do that I'd have to backtrack.

It's the writer's prerogative to rub out her tracks should they get stuck in claggy soil, but that's a cop-out benefitting only the reader who would not then see the moth underneath her muddy soles. And there will still be a dead moth on my desk, buried under the accumulated mass of other creatures I hadn't saved from a certain end other than by destroying the page describing their death throes. But this type of rescue is merely an illusion: they carry on dying in the garbage can anyway. So, in the forest, Heather touches her aching head and waits for me to allow the sun to rise and set time in motion again.

The author reigns supreme over the breadth of territory, and sometimes, like a god wracked by doubt but nonetheless persisting with a god's unavoidable cruelty, abuses a power she doesn't know how to use.

It's been pouring since dawn and, faced with the grey gloom surrounding me, I can't stop talking about the rain, the storm, the tempest. I'm convinced these climatic events will exert a profound influence on the narrative arc, because not a day passes without the perpetual changes of temperature in this country having an effect upon my way of reacting to the world, in other words on my mood — whether I am cruel, kind, or compassionate.

The summer before I met Heather was a rainy one. Clouds every day. Showers every day. *Could all this rain be for me*, I wondered stupidly one morning, as I stood hypnotized by the water overflowing the eavestroughs, like a deranged woman who believes a thunderstorm has burst due to the irrefutable need she feels for her heartbreak to be matched by something equally forceful.

And yet the rainfall was gentle. And I wasn't deranged. I simply considered the water as a present dropped down from the height of the clouds, a gift to anyone wanting to enjoy the touch of the sky and the summer on their face. Still, there were others who would feel suffocated by all this streaming water, and my joy was diffused with shame when I looked at the flooded garden and saw the pallid basil unable to take root in the sludge, and thought of the rotting hooves of the animals in the ruts of infertile fields, of the wounds the humidity was inflaming. Is it possible that all joy has, concomitantly, a dark and destructive side? Can I be happy only if other creatures suffer?

The water funnelled by the eavestroughs has furrowed grooves in the earth where the overflow pours out of the pipe, forming a network of channels snaking toward the road, that meet up in places before separating again when some obstacle deviates them from their course. I try to work out if one of the channels will become a river, and if the others, following the slope of the ground, will end up joining it, increasing its flow and enlarging its banks. Fascinated by all this surging, inflating, and swelling, by the water becoming a river in this miniature reproduction of the world, I wager that the ground will collapse two metres away from the cedars, forming a frenzied waterfall that will uproot the trees.

I play at God to align myself with his maleficence, that's what I say to P., who's reading a newspaper behind me. I can allow myself this seeming heresy, since gods are nothing more than inventions in man's own image, our true nature revealed more in war and abomination than in joy and lightness.

I play because I know kind gods do not exist, that they too are chimera forcing believers to imagine grand designs with infinite mercies hidden behind them, which are, however, only discernible to those capable of understanding the schemes in question. Which is to say nobody, and implicating in turn the gods themselves, concealing their kindnesses in plagues.

With my eyes fixed on the channel whose tributaries have slowly turned it into a rushing river, I add that if the gods weren't cruel, literature wouldn't exist, since there'd be nothing to write about except the benign satisfaction of the contented man. And then, through the roaring of the current, I hear the words "places, the cruelty of places," these spoken by P., who is looking at the rain. I remain at the doorstep as the storm winds of winter pass over and interfere in my landscape, forcing me to question the inexorable cruelty of the milieux in which the people I've created for my pleasure have to sleep and work—as do too, sometimes, those I see while I'm out walking, people who follow me because they have no other choice, because they can only exist if I do, and vice versa.

The gods I evoke, the destructive waters, this staring out at the world while under the spell of messages in the water streaming down the windows, all these images come to me from a movie I've almost entirely forgotten, apart from the overly staring eyes of a man who believes the raindrops diverging on a grey window announce a flood or catastrophe to be visited on the house. I am that crazy man. I am Heather Thorne.

Heather managed to get out of her car despite the bashed-in left door and the right side of the vehicle being angled down over the south slope of the hill and its tiny clearing. She picked up the axe lying on the back seat, left there by a helping hand or some man whose very existence she has forgotten—a lover, a father, a brother—and then wielded the tool horizontally, sharp edge toward her, and hit the window with all the might she could muster before wriggling outside, across pieces of glass forming a constellation of minuscule slivers clinging to the window frame, like a spider's web broken in the centre, a V-shaped shard attaching itself to her hair as she went through. Instinctively, she retracted her head into her shoulders, afraid another shard might dig into her neck and slice open her jugular, before exiting the narrow space into which the night wind was blowing, filled with smells of pine and fall, of dead leaves, stagnant water, and the urine of fleeing prey.

These smells reached her like a cloud of reminiscences in which she thought she'd identified a clue that might help her figure out who she was and where she came from—assuming, of course, that she might actually have come from somewhere other than the pile of crumpled metal from which she'd managed to extricate herself. She is barely conscious of belonging to a species that has learned to use names. Temporarily, Heather Thorne is nothing but pure instinct, pricking her nose up at the smells around her. The smells awaken in her the kind of animality that grips her right in the gut, tells her not to make a sound, and to watch out for the tiniest movement disturbing the still darkness. In the moment, Heather Thorne is no more than a lost spirit in a body whose suffering fades when compared with the whole disaster.

She licks her hands' open wounds and then covers them with moss and black earth. She performs the mechanical gesture without thinking, which links her to a form of knowledge someone has imparted to her in a past life already escaping her. The same thing happens when she stands up: she becomes a two-legged creature moving with difficulty in a direction that instinct alone tells her to take. Then she notices a light behind the hill; it's moving toward her, and behind it is another two-legged animal carrying a long stick made of wood and metal. *Gun*, she thinks. And in the dim light of the moon shining on the black metal, she remembers: the kind of animal I am is a woman, a creature that conceals her nakedness under skins not her own. And the animal approaching me is a man, a lone hunter, the kind of creature you find in novels.

The fall and its fogs have given way to winter. The furrows have frozen, the cold has asserted its rightful dominance and, in an hour or so, the clouds blown by the westerly wind will burst, parachuting a dozen centimetres of snow down upon our heads. This will make P. and I feel obliged to shovel a path to the road, and then others leading to the forest behind the house.

"Heather Thorne owes her survival to a simple logic which demands that a heroine cannot die before her story has begun. She owes her survival to me, to my needing her to exist if I am to continue inventing trees and women advancing between said trees, characters whose destiny will end in black ink suspending the *ennui* of cold days."

I write these sentences as a blizzard rages, slowly covering the paths P. and I dug earlier with more snow. The paths will have disappeared entirely before nightfall. We'll barely see anything more than their traces, where the curves of the paths have been polished by the wind, a few blades of hardened snow clinging to their edges.

The hill on the 4th Line is also covered in snow, but where Heather Thorne is standing it's still fall, still night, and still the hunter is moving toward her, his lamp trained on the face of the woman who has only just remembered what it means to be a woman. Heather and the hunter have not exchanged a single word. Not a single new leaf has touched the ground. No movement has been made.

Although it looks as though the man and Heather are anticipating a confrontation, in reality they aren't waiting for anything. For them, time has stopped, time during which they are not growing older, not thinking, not breathing. They are a picture painted on a timeless autumn night.

Moving on from this picture, a thousand scenarios are possible. I should choose only one, and follow its multiple digressions wherever the black ink flows. The route of my meandering is uncertain. I might have to retrace my steps and go back to the beginning of the forest in which Heather is not breathing. All the while I'm afraid the ink will stagnate and, as it soaks into the dog-eared edges of the page, force me to speed up events and modify the angle of the story in order to transport Heather to La Languette, where I'll have no choice but to give her the starring role in a tale of horror, the notes for which I sketched out last winter—days when I spent my Sunday afternoons walking up and down this isolated road, unaware that I'd soon be calling myself Heather.

In one of the scenes of this unfinished drama, a woman whose face I can't quite make out was walking in front of me, a woman whom it now seems impossible to call by anything other than my own name, Heather. She was walking briskly, her long blonde hair spilling out from under her red hat and flowing down her back. I could hear it rustling on the fabric of her coat, the sound of it alternating with the creak of her boots on the snow rendered shiny by the caterpillar tracks of passing snowmobiles. Their treads had dug an uneven chequered pattern, a network of cross-hatched lines that occasionally forced her to slow down so as not to lose her footing on the glistening patches.

Then two snowmobilers showed up, neither expecting

to see a young woman on their route, and both losing their heads when they saw her, ripping off her canvas coat and having to live with the repercussions of this madness for the rest of their days, each having nobody to whom they could admit their crime or their nightmares—except for the other man, the man at the very origin of the nightmare, whom they'd come to hate and could only tolerate on indolent nights when alcohol made them close again, united in the pathetic vulgarity of their overused jokes or, the opposite tendency, in the impetuous hurling of brash insults ripping out their guilty pasts and exposing them to the light.

The scene is all too familiar, in which all that is left of the young woman are some traces of blood on the snow, and all we see are the boots of the snowmobilers as they furiously kick snow over their tracks and wonder what the fuck has happened. "Gilles, tell me that didn't just happen, for Christ's sake tell me we didn't just do that!"

It's the kind of situation in which I could put an end to Heather without the story collapsing, because a new one would follow in its wake. The snowmobilers would take their turn in the spotlight, and then the people who went out to look for Heather—the young woman who went out walking when a blizzard was forecast and didn't come home for dinner, who'd not returned even as the clock's hands pointed to the heart of the night and emphasized the ineluctable passing of time.

The next question could be fatal for Heather Thorne: Do I really need her? Do I need Heather alive?

Not long ago, an injured squirrel climbed up to the cottage-shaped bird feeder swinging outside the patio door of my study, from which I watch the cedars blowing on windy days. The squirrel left traces of blood on the pale wood. Its foot must have been chapped by winter, by its severity.

I'll have to clean up the blood soon, since the mere sight of it makes my legs feel numb, as if I were the one feeling the pain of this squirrel, Ti-Boutte, and all the other red squirrels sauntering around morning to night from the maples to the feeder, from the feeder to the cedars, from the cedars to the fence that P. and I plan to reinforce in the spring so that it doesn't fall down beneath the weight of the wild rose bushes.

I'll have to put my gloves on to clean up the blood, though a trace of it will remain, just like what happened with the bombyx, a fine layer of brown powder delineating the fading shape of the moth's open wings on my desk. The stain from the squirrel's wound will become encrusted in the memory of the wood, changing from red to brown before becoming invisible, though that won't stop my leg muscles from tensing each time I see the feeder swinging in the wind.

Heather's blood didn't affect me quite as trenchantly, probably because her blood is also mine and Heather only bleeds if I do. I can't bear other people's blood. I can only come to terms with blood that emerges from wounds I inflict on myself, all of this amounting to nothing when compared with the suffering of creatures bruised by winter.

It's bizarre. Suddenly it seems as though I have memories that belong to Heather, of a little blue dress, a dog called Jackson, a white winter morning, intermingling with my own. I call to the dog running in the crazy snow, "Jackson, Jackson, my love," and look past the curtains of my blue bedroom to the landscape, and then I hear a yapping coming from Heather's forgotten childhood, followed by a cry of terror that throws me face down on the ground. The yell from La Languette. Heather Thorne's last cry.

When I come to my senses, the little blue dress is still there, laid out on the bed in a bedroom that is also blue. Heather's bedroom on a summer morning, a nagging question emerging from the filtered light: is my past becoming Heather Thorne's?

I close my manuscript as soft snow whirls in the cold air. The cat watches me from his armchair. He hasn't moved since this morning, hasn't eaten his fish, and didn't jump up to the window when a blue jay landed outside. Is he Heather's cat?

The night was long and dark but somehow I got through, my thoughts weighed down with intermittent dreams dominated by the grey of indistinct mornings. The curtains are grey, so too are the walls and the sky, which I surmise is overcast from the dusky light in the bedroom. I don't even know what time it is, what day even, or which season will set my mood once I open the curtains. I untangle myself from the crumpled sheets and look outside.

P. is there, in the middle of a path whose edges reach to his mid-thigh. Every time his bent-over body thrusts the shovel, the steam of his breath lifts in puffs around him. I imagine the muscles of his back contracting, the warmth of his skin, his sweat soaking into the wool despite the biting cold. We are in deep winter. I repeat: we are in deep winter. Only Heather Thorne is still living in the fall.

The man has taken another step toward Heather and she retreats, soon blocked by the tangle of branches. Nervously, she surveys her surroundings for an escape route, looking for some gap she might run through without having to hunch over and, in so doing, offer up her vulnerable back to the hunter.

Cornered into the rampart of trees on the north side of the clearing, Heather asks herself why she instinctively fears this man when actually she should be overjoyed by his unexpected appearance in the heart of the forest. He must know it well if he's walking through it in the middle of the night and perhaps, if she abandons the idea of flee-ing, he'll help her find her way, maybe offer her an arm to lean on. She has a searing pain in her right thigh, in the same spot where her ripped pants provide a view of blood drying on white skin, and the man must have noticed this pain in her pursed mouth and slight limp. So she waits for him to hold a hand out to her, offer her a drink from his water bottle, pull a clean tissue from one of his pockets so she can wipe away the blood slowly clotting on her right cheek—all entirely natural things to do when you stumble across an injured woman.

For a moment Heather holds her breath, because the evocation of women weakened by clearly visible injuries brings to mind an image lost in the fuzziness of the night, of a woman standing near a ditch and looking haggard, or stunned even, as if she's just come to grips with the meaning of an equation that has evaded her for so long, or just remembered where she put some object—a piece of jewellery or a letter—that she's been trying to find for weeks.

Heather has forgotten the details of this event, but remembers the way the woman smiled as she passed, a smile indicating she should continue on her way but which then froze, along with the rest of the woman's body, paralyzed by an astonishment suddenly giving way to a terror that had to be related to her journey along the deserted road.

For a moment, the man doesn't exist anymore. In the light of the gibbous moon, other images come to Heather Thorne: of the stranger's medusa smile and her purple leather jacket, the thin trickle of a stream disappearing in the ferns, the horizon line crosshatched by the waving treetops. Words bully their way through the images: *Gilles, tabarnak, tell me we didn't just do that*. And then, in the echoes of his crude *tabarnak*, Heather Thorne is struck by the truth confirmed by the gaze of the woman in the purple leather jacket: I am an injured woman and I am called Heather, I must be called Heather. And now, paralyzed in turn, she lowers herself back against a tree trunk in order to rest and repeats, "My name is Heather, Heather Thorne."

As she speaks these words, the man shines his lamp on Heather Thorne's face. Instinctively, she lifts her arms, blinded by the light and seeing only the black silhouette of the armed man in the yellow halo. Time has stopped, again, and they size each other up: two animals, one of which has encroached on the other's territory; two big cats unable to share the same space. Then, too fast to catch, a vague memory traverses Heather's field of vision at lightning speed, like a dream in fading colours. *I know this man*, she tells herself, she knows this man from a distant memory her current problems can't access. She plasters on a smile so that the man won't notice her discomfort and starts to move forward.

On the ground, a few steps away from the hunter, is Heather's axe, its blade glinting in the moonlight.

II.

Six months have gone by since my encounter with Heather, six months during which I watched the snow falling with a growing sense of oppression. Was the winter ever going to end, or had the northern hemisphere entered into a glacial age scientists had not anticipated, or had they, in league with the government, knowingly suppressed their knowledge of it? Had they feared panic and a mass exodus of the well-to-do invading countries south of the equator and decimating their populations? Had they foreseen a subsequent increase in suicides among those who didn't have the means to flee, and the resulting morbid spectacle of frozen hanged bodies swinging in the glacial July winds?

I couldn't stop these macabre scenes invading my thoughts whenever I thought about the cold's unrelenting power and my utter impotence in the face of its fatal effects. I watched days' worth of snow accumulate, and witnessed nights that got the better of another squirrel, of Ti-Boutte Côté or maybe Ti-Boutte Chouinard, of two or three more of the redpolls that were less and less plentiful at the feeders. I saw my own blue-tinged body swinging from a leafless maple, the maple which would never have leaves again, and I could not imagine how my life would be able to continue in permanent winter, how the house could be kept warm, and how our means of subsistence could possibly be enough to fight against walls of ice slowly encasing all living things.

Only the off-seasons do not aggravate my anxiety, transitional months without the extremes that constitute a threat—times like last autumn, for example, when I abandoned Heather and waited for the arrival of days proving to me that the natural order of the seasons hadn't been scuppered by some atmospheric phenomenon or planetary unravelling caused by humans' idiotic greed.

Those days arrived, slowly, and now here I am, on a day in which it seems possible to believe in spring's coming and the return of blackbirds and swallows. The streams are thawing now and still I could pick up my tale right where I left off and carry on with the scene in which P. is digging a path through the snow reaching up to his thighs, except that the scents of the coming summer are so insistent I can't quite conjure up a winter I so eagerly want to be over.

This story, I decided when I got up this morning, will be told in real time. In other words, I'm not about to drag out the winter just to avoid the lengthy pauses caused by chores that often interrupt the writing process, things like taking care of the birds and the cats, the pain and joy of my loved ones, all the things demanding the pen be put down and my eyes turned away from the work.

There's too little of my life left not to delight in the play of the light, its movements evident even in the words I'm writing in black ink: "sun and more sun, anemones and violets, laughter, bare feet on the burnt wood."

As for Heather's existence, that will also proceed in regular fashion, at the heart of a fall unspooling in parallel with other people's seasons.

Yesterday, P. and I finally repaired the fences. We straightened the posts, strengthened the cross rails, removed anything that was too damaged, and replaced the broken pickets with pieces salvaged from old sections. We made our presence felt on this parcel of land as it tried to slide back into chaos, an attempt at domestication that will only be apparent for a few weeks, until more parts of the fence are felled by bad weather, unruly grass has grown on the low hill covering the septic trench we dug to treat our waste water, and moss and weeds, despite our best efforts, have reached the flagstones by the house steps, bringing with them the soil in which they take root.

It takes so little—and so little time—for human constructions to fall into ruin, disintegrate, and disappear. The things we build lack the longevity of trees, trees that don't require repair or strengthening, and manage perfectly well without us; they lack the doggedness and determination of the wild roses that scratched my arms when P. and I were putting the fence back up on the section of the property adjoining the road. There, in mid-June, the gentle slope is covered with thorny bushes and their abundant pink beauty as soon as the flowers bloom, though we must stop them from multiplying if we don't want them to reach the house and attack it just as moss and grass have done the flagstones. It's like in one of those apocalyptic movies where concrete cracks open and roots push through, and walls collapsing under the weight of trees quietly return to earth.

I share my thoughts with P. as I clean the wounds on my arms, paying special attention to the M-shaped cut where my right wrist flexes, something that must have happened when I was picking up shards of glass from what had once been the house's garbage dump behind the old barn. The mark gouged into my flesh looks like the wound Heather got when she extricated herself from the car, and which then started to bleed as the hunter moved toward her — and toward the axe on the ground, its blade gleaming in the moonlight.

Heather's intention is to get hold of the axe and strike, if necessary, or use it to dissuade the man if he suddenly becomes aggressive, as happened in that jumble of images that flooded her mind of a young woman lying on the ground near a snow-covered path. *Tabarnak, tell me we didn't just do that.* But the man has noticed Heather's furtive look at the axe, and the plan visible in her glance, and so he picks it up and sends it flying into the woods behind him.

Without a word, he moves closer to Heather, staring at her face as if he's trying to recognize his own in it, and then, with trembling hands, he offers her his water bottle, holds out a tissue, looks her right in the eyes and murmurs, "You aren't who you think you are. You aren't Heather Thorne." Quickly, he looks away, adds that he'll call for

34

help, both for the car and her injuries, but Heather says no. The Buick is part of the scenery now, and there's no point trying to retrieve it. She can already see the brambles taking root, the rodents sheltering in it, the shell breaking down and rust mixing with clay.

Heather Thorne doesn't want help. She just wants to know the identity of this man who seems to have risen from a past the brambles are concealing, and why he claims the name that emerged from another woman's stunned face is not her own. So, arms dangling, she stays put, lost in the smell of the man's breath. It has a slight smell of juniper and reminds her of the joys of childhood.

It's bombyx time again. After the night when one of those insects died on my desk, I tried to immerse myself in the night-time world of moths, convincing myself that a writer ought to be able to name a creature dying right in front of her, but this universe is so complex, and my ignorance so vast, that I give up trying to identify the species currently hurling itself at my lamp. It's as likely to be a *Notodonta tritophus* as a black witch moth, and its evocative name might lead me into one of those stories where death hinges on the beat of a wing.

In any case, I've learned from my partial and disorganized reading that the word *bombyx* references a category that groups together various moths belonging to different families, from *Lasiocampidae* to *Notodontidae*, and that there are probably as many types of bombyx as there have been July nights since I was born.

So I drop my arms and resign myself to ignorance, preferring imprecision to a desire to name that could lead to obsession and fill my evenings with research distracting me from my principal preoccupations — getting to know Heather Thorne and the man she met in the woods. Ever since they met, I've been repeating over and over again what the man said to Heather: *You aren't who you think you are. You aren't Heather Thorne.* These words, spoken by a stranger whose appearance I'd not expected, disconcert me as much as they must have done Heather, because they also put my own identity into question, and even affect my ability to name whatever appears in my study when bombyx time comes around again.

Might I have been mistaken? Maybe the woman I saw at the wheel of the Buick on the 4th Line wasn't Heather Thorne, and I've borrowed some nameless woman's identity. Could it be that Heather Thorne is an imposter?

I look at my reflection in the window beyond the cat's armchair, the shape of my face imprecise and my pale lips stuck on the man's words, "You aren't who you think you are." I ask myself if the image in the window is true, if it's the reflection of the woman I believe I am. I move closer, lean toward it and, with my forehead pressed against the cold glass, smile at the woman disappearing in the steam of my feverish breath.

The man with the gun has just come out of the forest and is sitting in his truck, which is the same red colour as his shirt. He has both hands on the wheel and is lost in the dawn, staring at its first rays as they appear behind the slope where a sparrow hawk is gliding. "My name is Heather," the injured woman had said as she leaned against a tree. "Heather Thorne." But the man knows that's impossible. He only knows one Heather Thorne, a young girl whose skin is blemished from the thousand suns that used to warm the sides of the mountain overhanging the village, and the woman claiming to be Heather Thorne cannot be that young girl.

William Carlos Willams's *Paterson* sits on the black table next to my desk. A bookmark partway through reminds me I've not finished reading it yet. I started it during the winter, with the cat on my lap, snow and hail blowing against the windows, and each time my eyes drifted from the text I thought of Heather. I open the book to page 28, to where another bookmark placed across the page points my attention to a letter signed "E. D." that seems to stimulate my deliberations on my relationship with Heather. "With you," E. D. claims, "the book is one thing, and the man who wrote it another. The conception of time in literature and in chronicles makes it easy for men to make such hoax cleavages."

I don't know who E. D. is, since Williams doesn't bother to enlighten us as to the identity of his correspondents, but this doesn't really matter because the two sentences attributed to E. D. suggest to me it's actually Williams speaking, still and always Williams; who draws words from other sources, makes them his own and gives them new life within the architecture of *Paterson*. In the present example, it's neither E. D. nor Williams expressing themselves in the two sentences I've quoted, but I, Andrée A. Michaud, who am at one with my book; I, Heather Thorne.

The thick fog the wind drives up from the waterlogged earth is like blowing snow. Hair plastered to my temples, I move through the fog as trees and fields disappear ahead of and behind me. Alone in a cocoon of pale light whose shifting shape moves with me, it's impossible for me to guess what awaits beyond the slope or to touch the furtive shadows slipping in and out of the folds of the misty curtain covering my steps.

I've been walking like this since dawn, and in the damp silence calming my thoughts, I close my eyes from time to time, trying to distinguish the face of the man with the gun. Sometimes a set of features floats into view, the blue of an eye looking intensely my way, and then the blue dilutes into grey, carrying the rest of the face with it.

A vehicle approaches, and I can just about make out the headlights without being able to calculate how far away it is. I leave the road to get closer to the cries of a loon taking off from the water by the Martinique, an old restaurant and bar I visit now only in my memories. On the path through the bush around the lake, I sit down on a wooden chair that was perhaps abandoned by a reveller who'd used it to take in the breeze at the edge of this forest-ringed lake. I try to retrace the sequence of events from the moment when the man with the gun arrived on the scene, but I can't manage it.

So I scroll back up through the text and write it, again, until the word *gun* is tapped out on the keyboard and the loon takes off. *Gun*, she thinks. *Gun*. In the forest, Heather keeps an eye on the long metal and wood stick slung over the shoulder of the man approaching her, although she's still unable to see his face, nothing but a black oval behind the ringed halo of his flashlight. It's not until he comes closer that she can make out his high forehead, his smoothed-back hair, the wrinkles on each grizzled temple like the branches of an apple tree, and an uncomfortable feeling convinces her she knows this man.

The feeling becomes more concrete when the man locks eyes with her and the combination of his irises, blue encircled with yellow, and the heat of his breath imbued with sweet odour, catch on the edge of an old memory. I try to draw out the stare, and to discern what these smells anchored in Heather Thorne's childhood might be, but the spell is abruptly broken when the man turns his head away from her. His face becomes blurred, and the child-hood scents dissipate in an unanchored haze. Once again Heather is a woman alone and paralyzed by fear.

In the fog coming off the lake in thin curls, pierced now by the first rays of sun, all I make out are the outstretched wings of a bird of dawn and twilight, frightened by the over-loud clacking of a keyboard.

———

I took out my sketchbook and tried to draw an Identikit picture of the man with the gun. The face in front of me is that of Jeff Bridges in *The Big Lebowski*—which is utterly ridiculous. Unless, that is, Heather feels, as I do, a particular attraction to the ageing Hollywood actor and has substituted his features for those of the man with the gun, either to control her fear or to convince herself she's in some kind of imaginary universe in which all dreams are possible. Just like that woman who liked going to the movies on slothful days.

But fiction cannot rely on illusion more than it does on reality, or it will crumble as soon as the slightest tremor shakes it. What I must look for are the features of a man suddenly discombobulated by an unexpected autumn meeting deep in the forest; who is maybe wondering, as I am, what made him enter the forest in the first place.

I tear up my sketch of Bridges, open my manuscript to read over the latest pages, and pick up my pen.

Heather Thorne, still rattled by the man's words and preferring not to think too much about them, has applied more mud to the wounds on her hands and thigh and the join of her wrist. Right in a fold of the leather jacket that should have protected her a wide gash of unexplained origin reminds her of its existence every time she moves her arm. Then she turns around and takes shelter in her vehicle resting among trees that will soon take root in it, the smell of rust already forming. It's daytime now, and she limps her way out of the forest to the exact spot where she crashed just as a woman on the radio was announcing that the next day would be glorious.

The sun has just risen behind the hill, forcing her to blink in the light, so much brighter than the shadows in the woods. She looks down and notices the body of an orange and black caterpillar on the ground, one of those furry caterpillars children call woolly bears, but Heather Thorne has only adult words in her head. *"Pyrrharctia isabella,"* she murmurs. Isabella tiger moth. She cups the insect's body in the palm of her hand and surveys the gravel path. Three other caterpillars, two heading west and one east, are progressing slowly over the small stones; an exodus of caterpillars which, in another time, she would have called the caterpillar migration, a long and daring march toward hibernation. But today the weather seems conducive more to catastrophe than to the seasonal journeys of certain species. Heather knows the Isabella tiger moth is looking for a place to overwinter, but she can't stop herself imagining the cataclysm imminent in the death march of these insects almost certain to be crushed by vehicle wheels — as will thousands of other Isabella tiger moths also crossing roads beyond which they think they'll find shelter from the cold.

In the too-perfect silence, Heather is alive to the drama at odds with the gentle wind bearing the humidity of the season. And she can see it in the tracks left on the road by the vehicle of the man — *you aren't who you think you are* — tracks in which the caterpillar, *Pyrrharctia isabella*, was resting earlier.

"Like Heather, I've always been fascinated by the mass of caterpillars that can be seen crossing the road in both directions as soon as we reach mid-September, though also somewhat perplexed by this species migration, which strikes me, every time, as a suicidal impulse pushing *Pyrrharctia isabella* toward the warm expanses of bitumen where certain death awaits.

"This insect's appearance on our roads brings to mind the slow breakdown of a world in which survivors flee in silent chaos, and north and west no longer exist. It makes me think of the pointless dispersal of a handful of condemned people totally unaware of the imminence of a collision about to wipe out the earth and scatter its pulverized fragments among those of all the rest of the planets that are a testament to oblivion's eroding pace."

As I write this, I realize that Heather is encroaching on my territory as if she were absorbing me, the way an ischiopagus fetus absorbs its twin and creates a sickly creature that no longer knows which of its prior four hands belong to it and which is holding the pen.

I should be wary of Heather. She's one of those people who drags you into their orbit and makes you lose track of what's real, all the while dropping a trail of breadcrumbs in their wake — which the birds then peck away, the better to confuse you.

The scratches I got when I mended the sections of fence among the wild roses with P. are slowly fading. Fine pink lines—not to be confused with the harsh, defined cuts of a razor or a knife—mark my inner arms where the skin is so tender, but in a few days they'll have disappeared to make room for other scratches, the depth of which will show whether I've been cording wood, gathering branches, piling rocks at the edge of the property, or picking berries and caring little about getting scratched by the tangled raspberry canes.

The M-shaped wound on the bend of my wrist refuses to heal, however. I've put mud on it, as my mother taught me long ago, I've cleaned it many times and applied various creams, but the lesion's slightly fringed edges are still bright red under the glowing skin. This injury will leave a scar and be proof that my story is a true one, in which blood does not cede to the will of someone wanting to see it gone.

An unexpected storm battered our region, and summer seemed as though it were no more than a brief flow of hot air over the dusty roads. Ten or more centimetres of snow fell in the night, blown by a north wind we could hear whistling in the chimney.

Several more months have passed since I repaired the fence with P., several months of invisible days during which I feel as though I've been wandering alone on an arid plain, cut off from light, cut off from night, cut off from the blooming of the hydrangeas and asters. The summer has retreated into this disassociated time, and here we are back again at the point where P., his back all sweaty, is digging the path leading to the forest floor, head dipped forward to protect himself from the stinging hail. That April morning when I swore to myself in the dazzling spring brightness that I would wholeheartedly enjoy the colours of the coming season is now far behind me, lost deep in that infertile plain where I no longer exist.

In the area of the 4th Line to which her life is currently confined, Heather Thorne hasn't reckoned on things changing either. She didn't see the summer coming to an end, hydrangeas wilting, leaves turning red, phlox stiffening in the frost. She barely felt the rain pass over her injuries and imbue the ground with a scent of cold rottenness.

Since these months have been stolen from my senses, and I only have the memory of other summers to narrate, I plunge into the heart of the storm like someone wanting to run barefoot in the warm rain. I put P. into position on the path, focus on the whistling of the wind, and reread the page where Heather strokes the soft fur of a squashed insect.

Intending to turn back the way she came, Heather Thorne has abandoned the caterpillars to their fate. She stands at the top of the hill, at the point on the road along which she'd arrived, and cannot recall whether she came from the north or the east. Houses are dotted here and there by the intersection in the shade of the hill, but she doesn't recognize any of them. The second house on the right, the paint of its red shutters flaking, vaguely reminds her of a house she recalls being under the trees, except this one is surrounded by an enormous lawn where all she sees are wilted rose bushes. The house at the south corner of the crossroads would also have struck her as familiar, were it not for the barn behind it, a red-roofed building near which a child is playing hopscotch and singing, "One, two, buckle my shoe."

Heather looks at the child, and then at the big slope to the right, and decides she must have come from the section of the road that appears to be clinging to the foot of the mountain, its beauty receding in the fine fog. Contemplating the stunning view offering itself up to her, she feels that the errant can only really make progress in settings whose splendour has been designed to mitigate their sense of being lost. But she fears a trap, so, still following her instincts, sets off in the other direction.

The M-shaped wound where my wrist flexes is identical to the one I drew long ago on Sissy Morgan's skin. Sissy was a young girl who died from bleeding out when the jaws of a bear trap closed around one of her long legs. That happened not far from here, at Boundary Pond, before the winter caught me off guard.

Heather has just arrived at my house. I can see her through one of my study windows, where melting hail has mixed with the snow accumulating at the bottom of the panes and made shapes resembling mountainous landscapes dotted with greenish lakes. Heather stands, right leg slightly raised because of the pain, under the archway at the entrance opening onto our property. Above her head, the wooden plaque with our house number swings in the wind, making its rusty chains squeak.

Distracted by the squeaking, which stirs up old childhood fears, Heather doesn't dare go any further. The arch beneath which she's standing seems to cleave the world in two. To the north of the arch, it's still fall—indeed, some *Pyrrharctia isabella* are crossing the road behind her. But beyond it, snow is piled up on either side of a path that someone has recently dug out. A man, she guesses, judging from the size of the footsteps pressed into the snow. A shiver runs through her body and she sees me, standing at the window and signalling for her to come in.

I wonder why I've brought Heather here, because I have no idea what to do with her once I've opened the door. Incapable of deciding whether or not I was going to let her head toward the misty beauty of the mountain, I stupidly propelled her to retrace her steps while I was clearing the paths with P. or continuing my reading of *Paterson*. In fact, I don't even know why I wrote this incredibly simple sentence: "Heather has just arrived at my house." I was aiming for an effect of surprise, I think, the cymbal clash that would make readers start and hold their breath, but now I'm faced with a situation that both frightens and disconcerts me. What am I to do with Heather Thorne once she crosses the threshold and we are confronted with our resemblance?

From the other side of the archway, arms wrapped around her body, Heather begins to limp along the path dug out by P. She ought to run in this cold, but, like me, she's afraid of the meeting about to take place. She hesitates for a moment at the bottom of the porch steps, wondering if perhaps she shouldn't just turn around, retreat back through the arch and into the fall I've prolonged for her sake. This season, thinks Heather Thorne, could become her eternal fall, but the fear of being its captive and having to witness the trees slowly rotting pushes her forward.

47

With my hand on the doorknob, I too am questioning myself. Should I open it, or send her back out into the woods, back into a restricted universe where her fate has only a distant influence over mine, following a plan in which our lives play out in parallel?

I could take Boris Vian's famous sentence in the preface to *Froth on the Daydream*: "This story is entirely true because I imagined it from one end to the other," but this would be a lie, in part, my story only "entirely true" because I have *lived* it from one end to the other.

I push the door open and wave Heather in.

Heather is sitting in the cat's armchair, the cat having fled after I opened the door and let in a gust of glacial air. I'm sitting at my desk opposite Heather, with about a metre between us. Were we both to lean forward with outstretched arms, our fingers could touch, like in those movies when one of the characters is desperately reaching out and someone grabs his hand before he falls down, and down, with no way back.

I've lit the lamp near where the memory of the bombyx lies, and its glow is cutting Heather's face in two, just as it must be dividing mine. If we brought together the two illuminated parts of our faces, we might finally see what the real Heather Thorne looks like — the one existing only in our amalgamation. As for the shaded parts, they seem to want to flee toward the windows so they can disappear into the night that suits them more than the overly bright light.

Heather's been here for over an hour and still hasn't said a word. She's looked at her surroundings and scrutinized me, observing the scratches all over my arms and pausing on the M-shaped wound on my right wrist. And she's taken little sips of the tea I made for us. When she opens her mouth, it will be to ask me who she is, where she comes from, and whether or not I've arranged a future for her, or if we're condemned to sit and stare at each other until her face disappears as mine is superimposed over it.

P. has just come down the stairs and noticed us, Heather and me; two women with identical profiles sitting face to face in my study. He asks why I haven't come up to bed — why I'm still down here in the half-dark watching a character who, regardless, will be coming to bed with me — but I indicate that he should leave us alone. Heather and I must see our silent meeting through. Sighing, he goes back upstairs, clearly not understanding my determined efforts to discern my features in the shadowy ones of a woman who, according to P., I have entirely fabricated — even if she's every bit as real as the story I'm living through these pages.

We can hear P. snoring, aware even in his sleep that he is not just my companion now, but also Heather Thorne's.

Heather and I eventually compared our injuries, and as we brought our arms back to our bowed bodies, we felt the light dimming as the room's temperature dropped, as if the anguish emerging from the identical nature of our injuries had pressed with all its weight down upon the house's atmosphere. Even our faces seemed no more than lunar-white half-ovals from which every distinguishing mark had disappeared. We needed nothing more for us to understand that we were linked by a kinship stronger than blood, and this bond would remain, whether we liked it or not, until one or other of us left the stage.

But, aware we should not have met each other yet — that we risked becoming a single formless entity condemned to stasis — Heather quickly asked me what kind of future I had planned for her, but I had no answer to give. As I've already said, how can we predict what, tomorrow, a storm or mere gust of wind might set off, what might prompt an unexpected phone call, or cause a branch to snap with such a startling crack that I'm inspired to head toward the source of the sound and entirely forget the text I've been hunched over in my effort to lose myself in the colours of winter. How can we predict the consequences of her limp, when it might lead us in an altogether unexpected direction and have us reinvent everything — from her accident right up to the moment of her meeting the man with the gun.

In any case, we had to start there, with the man with the gun, before the effects of the cold could distract us from our endgame and leave us to fate. We needed to find this man again and work out the meaning of his words, *You aren't who you think you are.* Our future and reality depend on it.

Out of the silence Heather had fallen into since I'd started to speak, I heard a low murmur. It might have been agreement. To echo her distress, I murmured in turn, then waited until she'd put her cup down on the corner of my desk before asking her to leave and never come back. We'd see each other again, but in territory where our faces could not be erased by the light.

Heather has just made her way back through the arch, on the other side of which leaves are spiralling down in an autumn night that's not yet known the snap of frost, and I'm alone in the sleeping house with no chance of abandoning myself to dreaming.

I touch the M-shaped wound reddening my right wrist and wonder what led to it. Did this letter so deeply encrusted in my flesh come from the rose bushes, from Sissy Morgan, or from Heather Thorne? Do I project my own injuries onto people around me, or, through some strange phenomenon of wishful thinking, do they appear on my skin like stigmata of the alienation of an author unable to separate her flesh from the written word?

If this is the case, then before long my body will be entirely tattooed with the miseries fiction inflicts on the characters it creates in its effort to give reality meaning.

Andy Williams, may he rest in peace, is singing "It's the Most Wonderful Time of the Year" on the radio, and I let myself be carried away by the nostalgia of a time so distant I can scarcely remember being the little girl who trembled as Christmas approached, plunging joyfully into the Sears and Eaton's catalogues full of every single thing that could satisfy the desires of spoiled children unaware that this greed would partly determine their ridiculous adult dreams. Christmas is a few days away, but I don't feel the slightest hint of excitement. On the contrary, I am dreading the tedium of long white nights during which I'll have to fake joy with a few guests who'd no doubt prefer to be sitting comfortably in their own living rooms and watching the year's latest blockbuster.

Despite this total absence of spirit, I went up to the attic with P. to look for our few Christmas decorations, hoping the sight of our artificial mistletoe wreath would ignite a spark that would help me remember the meaning of the holiday. A wasted effort: it has no meaning left. If only we were able to celebrate the solstice and be seduced by some pagan rite, if only we could sing about the advent of some hypothetical saviour, but all we do is prove that a commercialism we disapprove of has conquered our will and is therefore doubly victorious.

P. agrees with me on this point. He watches me hang my golden owls above the kitchen table and wonders why the tacky figurines compel me to hum "It's the Most Wonderful Time of the Year" despite my not believing in any of it. I haven't admitted to him how deeply attached I am to these night birds I've named Crappy and Holy Junior—this, in memory of the one and only Holy Crappy Owl, who has swung in my study ever since Marnie Duchamp, a character from one of my earlier novels, started talking to the straw bird. Nor have I let him know that, like Marnie, I talk to owls. P. smokes his pipe in the living room and watches me skeptically, choosing to remain quiet rather than repeat yet again that he doesn't understand why it is I waste my time with these few pathetic wreaths when, before the Three Kings even make it here for Twelfth Night, I'll have packed them back in their box the second I'm filled with the desire to hang myself right alongside Holy and Crappy.

He's right—the urge to hang myself, or to lie down in the snow and sulk, is as fervent as my desire to resuscitate a happiness I'm too old for now. Still, I persevere stubbornly and try to think back on the Sears catalogue from the winter of '67, in which the box of Lego I so desperately wanted was photographed next to the orange tractor my brother received on the twenty-fifth. And I try to forget these trinkets were simply prefiguring the cheap decorations I'm now wrestling with. Our nearest neighbour battled his yesterday, climbing his pine tree to adorn it with red lights that will flash in the dark until the moment when he, too, wants to cut the wretched thing down, cursing Jesus and the whole damn holiday season.

I tuck the Sears catalogue away in a corner of my memory and focus on the cold days when I'd shut myself away in my bedroom, on the second floor of the family house, and write as I watched the frozen larch and birches in the backyard while the others chatted downstairs. I have an unadulterated memory, one both sweet and nostalgic, of the moments when I'd leave the party and, cocooned in its warm murmur, fill up notebooks that will forever stay at the bottom of a drawer but nonetheless contain the entirety of my happy solitude. Perhaps this is the reason why, this morning, I'm breaking my back in order to balance a sparkling moose against the lamp in the hall. I want to recreate those hours during which, with my eyes riveted to the village cemetery half hidden in the frosty trees, I was preparing for the arrival of Heather Thorne.

I finally decided to go and visit V., an old friend who'd built himself a house on the mountain, because if anybody can tell me something about the man with the gun, it'll be V., who's never lived anywhere but in this area, and who knows, better than anyone, the woods and the people who frequent them: fishers, hunters, trappers, campers, walkers.

As soon as he saw me approaching, V. opened his front door with the same wide smile that seems not to have left his lips since he was a teen, the only difference being that now it reveals the network of wrinkles that age and his exposure to strong cold winds have engraved on his face. I saw, in his smile, all those years in which a bunch of us would hike to the mountains, to La Languette or any of the other places that constituted our domain, a territory bordered only by our desire to confine ourselves in it. Suddenly I want to throw myself into V.'s arms, as if coming across an old friend I'd thought dead, or whom I was leading back to the daylight after interring him in a damp vault for decades. Where had we been all those years? What kind of detachment had we withdrawn into?

Out of reserve, I modestly kissed V. on both cheeks and followed him into his enormous kitchen filled with the smells of nicely browned bread and tobacco. He made me a cup of coffee and then, as we sat around his wooden table, we picked up the thread of old memories, since nothing linked us more than the past—and neither of us understood how it had slipped away from us quite so easily.

When it came time to leave, I'd almost forgotten the main reason for visiting: the man with the gun. I questioned V. about him, but since my description of the man was somewhat vague, V. wasn't a great help to me. "It's like you're describing a dead man," he said finally, and I felt my head go numb, my feet and legs too, and my heart start to race. V. had hit the nail on the head. I'd just sketched out a ghost. And yet, the man with the gun couldn't be a phantom. If that had been the case, I'd have recognized him— a writer always knows her ghosts. Noting my uneasiness,

V. suggested that perhaps it was Casgrain. Maybe Casgrain or Ferland, two guys from the next village who both had red trucks, though Ferland was a bit too young to match the man I'd described.

"It would be easier if you'd written down the licence plate," V. added, and I realized that I hadn't really seen the armed man's truck, and the only reason I knew its colour was because the man sat there after he'd left the woods, to reflect on his meeting with the woman claiming to be Heather Thorne. And I'd only witnessed this scene because the man with the gun had, to a point, written it.

A new rush of tingling travelled from my legs up to my neck. I stammered my thanks to V. and we promised to get together soon for a hike in the mountain trails like we used to. But, as I watched his silhouette shrink in my rear-view mirror, I was certain this hike would never happen. I would see V. again, but for other reasons that somehow, confusedly, I knew were linked to the man with the gun.

While P. was making dinner and John Coltrane's sax doing all it could to drown out Andy Williams's voice, which had insinuated itself into every corner of the house, I looked up Ferland and Casgrain's addresses in the phone book with every intention of going to the neighbouring village in the morning to see what these men looked like. Then I wrote out, on a blank page, the names of all my ghosts — from characters in my novels to flesh-and-blood people buried in the village cemetery situated in the hollow of the green or white rectangle, depending on the season, that I could see from my childhood bedroom. Then I reconstructed their faces, one by one, but none matched that of the man with the gun. Not a single one.

Heather, back now at her departure point, has proceeded down the hill to take a closer look at the houses around the crossroads. The little girl she saw the other day is still there by the barn, playing hopscotch and humming a nursery rhyme, quite as if she'd been invented to live in the scene eternally. As she jumps, she endlessly repeats the chant, "One, two, buckle my shoe," wearing red sandals that vault her toward the sky in a few jumps, then, "Three, four, knock at the door," after which she walks back around the rectangle she's traced in the gravel to begin again, "One, two, buckle my shoe."

Heather stays some distance back, worried her presence will frighten the child and break the spell that somehow keeps her alive. Then she sets off on the section of road that leads to the foot of the mountain.

Initially, she has the impression she's in an unknown territory, but then, little by little, the landscape clears up, branches part, and the tall grass bends flat to reveal hidden aspects of the scene. She recognizes the copse to the left of the road, although the trees in it seem bigger to her now, and a larch has appeared to the right of the birch among the cherry trees. The embankment on which the trees are growing haphazardly is less visible, and it looks more like a natural hillock than a pile of stones heaped up in the middle of a field by means of a plough and sweaty horses, whose glistening muscles must have exuded a strong animal odour mixing with the smell coming off shirtless men puffing and panting behind them. As for the many potholes in the gravel road, they sink even deeper where underground water loosens the ground. A bank of wild roses has moved closer to an old rail fence, and will end up invading the road if nobody prunes it.

The set has shifted, thinks Heather, though the landscape is mostly the same. If she were able to run, she'd sprint down the slight slope ahead of her and end up by a river — that, she suspects, would be lined by bigger trees, new bushes, and new grass — but her injured leg stops her.

She mumbles, "What if time got away from me when my car shot into the forest? What if, imperceptibly, I've moved with the set and am not who I think I am?" Then she sits down on a rock and stares at the mountain, which, at the heart of this moving scene, is its only immutable element. "I come from there," she tells herself. "I come from that mountain." But from her vantage point, she can see no house or building to indicate that anybody actually lives on the mountain.

My first intention, when I got up this morning, was to head to the next village and lie in wait for Ferland and Casgrain as they left for work, but I'd forgotten I had to help P. make *fiadoni*, a specialty of the Italian side of his family, for Christmas dinner. My little reconnaissance mission would have to wait until people arrived home from work — assuming, that is, that Ferland and Casgrain worked outside the house and weren't on holiday the day before Christmas Eve.

I spent a portion of the day smearing butter on baking trays, breaking eggs, putting *fiadoni* in the oven, and then paced back and forth as the smell of flour and cheese permeated the house. At four thirty I pretended I needed to run an errand and set off down the road. Darkness had already fallen, which could be an advantage overall, since Heather and I had only seen the face of the man with the gun in the dead of night, suffused with moonlight as the glowing clock in the Buick showed half past twelve. The sight of his face exposed in full daylight would likely scramble his features forever.

I started with Casgrain, who lived at the edge of the village, and whom it would be easier for me to monitor without appearing suspicious. His house was in total darkness. The curtains were drawn, the red and white bulbs running along the roofline were turned off, and an air of desolation peculiar to empty houses surrounded the stucco walls. Except for the driveway having been completely cleared of snow, everything pointed to Casgrain's having been away for some time. Nonetheless, I parked on Main Street — as far away from a streetlamp as possible — and sank back in my seat after I'd turned off the engine.

I was about to light a cigarette when a red truck pulled into Casgrain's driveway. A burly man with sagging shoulders jumped out and went around to help his passenger, a small woman who was even more bent over, navigate the footboard without tripping. As he leaned over to hold the woman's arm I was able to discern Casgrain's head and scrutinize his face for long enough to know that he wasn't my man. I felt vaguely disappointed, because the coldness of this house seemed to suit the solitude in which I imagined the man with the gun ought to live.

It was nearly five thirty when I came to Ferland's property at the end of the 6th Line. As I drove past the house, which was flanked by an enormous pine decorated with multicoloured bulbs flashing in the darkness, I noticed his truck was still in the drive and a silhouette was pottering about in what must have been the kitchen. I did a U-turn, drove back with my lights off, and parked a few metres away from the front door.

Aside from the multicoloured pine tree, the only source of illumination in this isolated corner was from the lamp-post installed near Ferland's garage. Waiting for Ferland to show, I pondered the deserted fields where dark tracks left by the passage of a few deer stood in the brilliant white-ness, as if the snow were somehow reflecting the light it had absorbed during the day. The memory of winter nights when I'd distance myself from the village in order to better feel the silence of those hours when the snowy owl soars, to think tranquilly and at my leisure, superimposed itself on the deer tracks. Numbed by the cold slowly creeping into the car, I lapsed into dreaming.

I was walking through the powdery snow when I was wakened from my light reverie by three knocks on the car door vigorous enough that some field mice, their shadows elongated by the full moon, bolted away. Framed in the middle of the window was the heavyset face of a furious-looking man. I let out a cry, more like a strangled sigh, and my first reflex was to lock the doors and drive off in order to put as much distance as possible between me and the sinister-looking giant and save myself. But then I remembered: Ferland, the man had to be Gilles Ferland.

I sat up straight in my seat and adjusted my coat, trying to hide my astonishment and unsure of what attitude to take. The man whose enormous fist was now banging on the roof looked exactly like one of the snowmobilers of La Languette. He was like one of those husky guys whose features I'd imagined one winter evening as I was laying out the foundations of a never-written novel in which a young woman is brutally murdered. I knew Gilles Ferland, and Gilles Ferland was not the man with the gun — but he *was* one of the La Languette murderers.

We stared each other right in the eyes for a few seconds, and then I lowered the window, not knowing yet whether I was going to apologize, find some way of justifying my presence at the end of the 6th Line of Saint-Vital in the bitter cold, or simply ask Ferland what he was playing at.

I didn't have to wonder for long, because before I'd had the chance to say a word, Ferland told me to get the hell out of there and never come back: "I never want to see you here again, is that clear?" No, it was not clear, but I was too upset to protest, and all the more so as a teenager and a slightly older young man were watching me from Ferland's big living room window, their gazes as piercing as Ferland's. There was also a small woman with black hair, no doubt Ferland's wife, arms crossed defiantly under her bosom.

I turned my head away, so much did the scene seem unreal to me, pressed on the gas pedal, and drove a couple of kilometres before stopping, alone in the darkness and in the middle of the icy road, and murmuring, "You aren't who you think you are, you aren't who you think you are, you aren't who—"

Then I opened the car door and went to throw up in the ditch.

The cat is sitting in his armchair, one half of his body illuminated by the lamp. Our second cat, a three-legged alley tomcat nobody wanted and whom we took in before moving away from the city, has just come downstairs for the night. He's emptied the first cat's dish of food, as usual, and has come to lie down on the mat by the door in my study that leads outside. Both of them are gazing at me, perhaps wondering why I'm so still and pale, or maybe they detect some anomaly in the human aura that cats can apparently see. Mine probably does have some unusual colour or glow—because I'm still caught up in my encounter with Ferland, as P. also perceived. When I got back home, P. was beside himself with worry, as I'd ostensibly gone out just to pick up a few croissants for tomorrow's breakfast. But when he saw my face he understood that something had happened.

As I'd been too stunned on my drive back from the 6th Line to consider that P. might be worried, I hadn't prepared an excuse. I told P. that I'd had car trouble, that there'd been an alarming flapping sound under the hood — the fan belt, which urgently needed to be replaced — but he didn't believe me. Just as the cats don't believe me even when I keep telling them everything's fine, when I tell them to sleep soundly instead of staring at me as if they've just seen a person returned from the dead. The place I've been is one they don't know, one of those lands of the real that only exist by virtue of fiction.

How to explain this to a cat? How to explain it to P. without him starting to wonder about the extreme states triggered by fatigue, or the long-term effects of fiction on the fertile imagination, when I don't know myself if I'm losing my mind, or whether I might have invented the man sharing my life and, in so doing, affirming that I am mad?

It's night again in Heather Thorne's universe. Around her, otherwise silent trees occasionally let out a sinister creak, and then everything quietens down again but for the insistent voice of the girl ahead of her — "one, two . . . one, two . . ." — the voice of the girl playing hopscotch, hammering its beat into Heather's thoughts with unrelenting regularity: *one, two . . . one, two . . .*

Heather tries to ignore the voice and takes a few small steps forward, afraid of waking an animal, of prompting some roaring maw, or one of those pale faces from her nightmares, to come surging out of the darkness. All the while she's wondering what possessed her to want to climb the mountain at all when the light was fading. She notices a rocky outcrop ahead of her and decides to stop there and wait until dawn before setting off again, but the voice wants to draw her further on, past the rock and to the higher reaches of the mountain, where its echo reverberates in the damp air.

"Enough," she mutters, "enough," but the little voice keeps on. "One, two . . . one, two . . ." *Enough.* Then Heather starts to sing too, she sings anything, singing just to drown out that crystal clear voice. And the shimmering voice rises further away, "One, two . . ." and the rhyme becomes no more than a barely audible chirping before it finally disappears on the far side of the mountain.

Heart pounding, Heather kneels behind a bank, convinced she's awoken the animal she was afraid of, but she hears nothing. At this hour, the forest seems to be populated only by its smells, of pine and fir needles, damp cedar wood, and she inhales them the way you would some nostalgic memory. Then she feels a hand slip into her own; it's rough, a man's hand, that of her father leading her into the woods. She tries to hold on to it, but the hand slips away again just like the face that appeared briefly along with the scent of the cedars.

On the verge of tears, Heather Thorne closes her eyes and focuses. She concentrates with all her might, and tries to conjure up a smile around which a face might materialize, but the face remains in a foggy cloud of unknowing, like that which, in certain television reports, accords anonymity to both criminals and victims.

With the passing of this vague recollection, Heather

Thorne's father, in her erased memory, ceases to exist, but for the remembrance preventing her from disappearing into the black abyss of the man with the gun—a simulacrum of memory ensuring her survival and fragmented identity.

Her eyes are wide open now. She wipes her forehead and tries once more to remember, but all she can see is a hand and a veil of fog.

In the distance, a little girl sings, concealed by the darkness that eventually silences her.

Day is breaking and I haven't moved. All night I wondered if my nerves had deluded me, if Gilles Ferland really did resemble one of the two attackers who emerged out of the snow in La Languette. Exhausted, I tried to interpret the meaning of his words, and figure out exactly whom he was talking to. When he'd ordered me never to return, had Gilles Ferland addressed the stalker shamelessly spying on his family through the windows of his house—or the author who'd endeavoured to turn his life upside down?

I try to convince myself that my first hypothesis was the right one—that Gilles Ferland resembled one of the two snowmobilers from La Languette: a coincidence impossible to explain. Perhaps, not long after I'd moved back to the area, I'd seen this man at the Saint-Vital post office or grocery store and had been struck by his appearance, the intensity of his gaze—enough so, that when I wrote the character of one the men from from La Languette, I'd subconsciously given him the features of the stranger

I'd come across on the very day that, without being aware of it, I was about to start a new story.

I ask the cats what they think. They dozed off a few hours ago and are only now beginning to rouse themselves. The first answers me with a yawn, and is amazed to see me still at my desk. The second pads upstairs to take refuge under my bed, and is just possibly still under the impression, perhaps, that I am not who I think I am, but a ghost who has returned from the dead to take the real A. A. M.'s place.

In a few moments, P. will come downstairs. First I'll hear the squeaking of the floorboard he steps on every morning after he wakes, followed by the sound of the toilet flushing, and then the creaking of the stairs. P. will appear in his red and black checked dressing gown and come to kiss me and ask if I had a good night. I won't admit that I didn't sleep a wink, and that a ghost — on reflection I'm sure it must have been a ghost — invaded my life yesterday. No, I'll pretend nothing is bothering me, and eventually I'll haul myself out of my chair to feed the cats, make coffee, and hustle us along in our holiday preparations — for tonight, December 24, is to be our night of festive celebration and disingenuous fake good cheer.

Heather left the mountain, because nothing seemed to want to keep her there, with the idea of finding shelter as she waited for some unanticipated event to disrupt her wanderings — for a flock of geese to cleave the air, or for some cold wind hinting at snow to show her fall is coming to an end.

Just as she was on the point of giving up, having let herself drop to the foot of a tree, planning to wrap her arms around it until morning to shield herself from fear, she noticed a cabin with an ATV parked outside it. Instinctively, she hid behind a stand of alder trees, while a voice coming from she didn't know where superimposed itself over the little girl's, *Tabarnak, tell me we didn't just do that, Gilles, tell me.* A moist warmth trickled down her temples as if two wet hands had just been placed there. Heather pushed the hands away, "Jesus Christ, just leave me alone," and curled in on herself, adopting the position fear demands when you feel vulnerable.

After a few minutes a man came out of the cabin, making Heather curl up even more tightly, mounted the ATV and started down a trail that must have led to the road. Heather waited a little longer, both to calm down and to be sure the man wasn't coming back, and then she went into the cabin, which still smelled of sweat and the dry wood stacked in a corner. Quickly she found a first-aid kit containing what she needed to tend to her injured thigh. She took some bandages, ointment, and peroxide, slipping the whole lot into a big backpack along with crackers, almonds, and a few tins of soup.

The sun is about to set and Heather, returning to her car, examines the bandage around her thigh, which has a little red stain that shows the blood hasn't yet coagulated. She covers the spot with the wool blanket she also stole from the cabin, and then stretches out on the back seat and shivers. The night wind muscles its way into the old

Buick and, as the light drops, she can hear the creaking of branches and the little noises made by animals beginning to hunt.

Holy and Crappy Junior, their feathers ruffled, swing above the table where the remains of the meal are piled up with the empty glasses and dirty dishes. Our guests left a few moments before, to the sounds of "It's the Most Wonderful Time of the Year," and the place seems oddly empty. Unaware of my discomfort, Holy and Crappy are still chattering on, keyed up from the excitement of the meal. P. has gone out to help our friends clear the driveway, because for the entire evening, fluffy snow that might have been specially created for Christmas has been slowly falling. I am alone with my coffee.

I think of Heather, equally alone in her car, who does not know that for a large part of the world, a saviour was born this night. Holy Crappy Owl, on whom the irony of my thoughts has not been lost, is hopping about on his perch squawking *bullshit, bullshit, this is all bullshit. Bullshit*, the two junior owls repeat in unison, *bullshit, bullshit, bullshit*, amused by the sound of this word whose vulgarity they only half comprehend. Then they wish me a merry Christmas, just as P., his beard white and cheeks red, comes into the house, bringing in with him a soft breeze in which a few Christmas flakes are gently twirling.

Sundays as they used to be lived had the advantage of compelling us to slow down, whereas today, we no longer dedicate any day of the week to the rest that mind and body demand.

On Sunday mornings, when other obligations don't force me to leave the comfort of my study, I sink into the slowness of that earlier time. I sit in my old cracked leather armchair, between the cat's seat and one of the windows looking out onto the woods, and open one of the poetry collections piled up on my black table or the bookshelf: E. E. Cummings, Nicole Brossard, William Carlos Williams, Renaud Longchamps, Paul-Marie Lapointe, Emily Dickinson, Roger Des Roches, Louise Dupré, and so many more. I dive into the heart of words summoned up to counter the futile agitation of people who fear what the silence they have thrown themselves into will reveal, and reflect, with Brossard or Longchamps, on the nature of man and rock.

I have just finished *Entre moi et l'arbre*—"Between Me and the Tree"—by Jean Sioui, a Wendat author whom I knew as a student during my single year of teaching, then as a spokesperson for his people. He's someone I respect for his proud humility. I underlined certain passages in the collection, to come back to them another Sunday, but for now repeat these lines:

> The greatest tremors
> Are born of the spectacle of forests.

This is what Heather, who has left her car to walk around, also thinks. She feels the shivers that come from both the beauty of the forest and the mysterious aura emanating from the apparently random arrangement of the trees its density grows. She experiences a state of grace, alongside the shuddering familiar to those advancing toward the essence of what they cannot understand.

I walk alongside her in the majesty of the fall, and am carried away by the peaceful feeling of the falling leaves, and then I leave Jean's collection of poems at the foot of a tree, so that some hiker equally fascinated by the beauty of the forest can lean against its trunk and feel the weight of the sap beneath the bark as he reads. With my lungs full of fresh air, I come straight back to my leather armchair, where the cat is waiting to settle in my lap and let me carry on with the idea of the forest as I pet his belly, eyes closed over his animal heat.

The terrifying infinity of the world pushes me to hope that I am wrong to think that there is no omniscient, omnipotent force breathing in synchronicity with the universe. I focus on this breath, one that inhales and exhales galaxies, that is like the ebb and flow of the oceans, and try to imagine what propels it—what movement, what other calm ocean, surrounds it. Blinded by the constancy of the stars, I balk every time before this incomprehensible being called God, this being who perhaps has no other name than the terror eternity evokes in me.

I look at the forest, beyond which I know there are fields, another forest, and a town, all of which are arranged on the curve of a circle that closes around the first forest, and wonder about the nature of the night that embraces the universe. Does it give way to another night, then another and another, or does this darkness shelter the white gaze of a god whom too much light would kill, just as it would destroy all obstacles to its spreading? And would the light recreate, in this way, an eternity of which it would be the all-powerful god?

When does a line end? What can you expect to find beyond a circle, if not another circle?

It's freezing on the 2nd Line, and I envy Heather the warmth of a fall in which, wearing only a leather jacket, her neck exposed to the sun peeking through the trees, she can come and go without a scarf. Not wanting to go mouldy in her damp vehicle, she sets off on one of the daily walks she now has to force herself to take. Besides, she thinks, she's started to smell the rot, a kind of green odour clinging to her skin. She thinks her limbs might end up falling away from her body one by one—as if she were already dead, as if she were experiencing the process of her own putrefaction.

She sits on an old stump whose moss she's scratched off with her blackened nails, rests her elbows on her knees, and stares into the distance. Then she leaps up and shouts, *What am I doing here? What am I doing in this damn forest?* She waits for an answer to push her out of her torpor, because she knows that one fine day a man, a woman, or an animal will walk around the car in which she is sheltering and alter her destiny. I don't yet know the face of this man, woman, or animal. In fact, I don't even know if it will be a living creature or a storm, a sudden squall, that will abruptly put an end to Heather Thorne's too-slow existence. I don't know because the cold that has paralyzed the 2nd Line for weeks has plunged me into lethargy, and even evoking the fall cannot shake it off.

The cold is killing me and I don't understand how, year after year, we survive its repeated attacks of frost; how the birds that plunder the feeders every morning manage to get through the glacial nights in which snow squeaks underfoot and freezes in drifts that take on the texture and appearance of rock. Only the faint hope of a kinder sun keeps us above the surface of this whiteness. And, perhaps, rage—the rage of a gusty wind piling the snow on branches that bow, lean, and swell, before projecting powdery clouds that look like the mists of some violent paradise.

III.

The man with the gun lives on the other side of the mountain. The man with the gun is called H. W. Thorne.

Thirty-eight words. That's all I managed to write yesterday after following H. W. Thorne's truck. Thirty-eight words that boil down to this: "*The final straight* is a phrase that has always chilled me to the bone, because it prefigures death, the final hour, the final space we travel through before the endless blackness. The final straight hurtles into the darkness."

My intention, when I wrote the first three words of this fragment, was to write about the book or film that is called, in my memory at least, *Final Straight Before Death*, and to allude in it to the numbness that takes over my legs every time we leave the crossroads on our way home from the neighbouring village and set off up the last portion of the straight road before we get to our house. This is when a single question consumes my mind: will *this* final straight be *my* final one?

But tiredness stopped me, an exhaustion commonly preceding the task of having to explain everything this expression means for me. The ambition of words, when it exceeds my ability to grasp it, leaves me feeling profoundly defeated. Which is what happened yesterday when I was confronted with this final straight, which had suddenly taken on a cold metallic hue.

If I had continued, I'd have ripped up my manuscript and scattered the shreds outside. So, instead, I put my pen down and picked up, from the pile of magazines lying on my black table, the latest issue of *Country Living*, flicking through it until I found a picture to distract me from the steel blue of the final straight. Then I looked at the sea through the window, its curtains blowing in the wind. I looked at the sea and dived in, salt filling my mouth, sun filling my eyes, since, in any case, I'd been unable to remember the paltriest scene or line from the movie, or was it a novel, whose title had once gripped me to such an extent that every attempt to work out what it had awakened in me made me feel nauseous.

Seeing me frozen over the magazine's glossy pages, P. suggested that I go out and get some fresh air. He was right. I needed to exit the smoky atmosphere of my study — and fast — to escape both the rigour of words and a seclusion that would end up suffocating me. Since the cold was still clinging to the countryside, I jumped into the car and headed to the 4th Line, a road I'd not travelled for a long time, its winding curves allowing me to forget that a straight line can lead to death.

I had just started driving around the first bend when I spotted the red truck in the exact same place it had been parked when Heather came out of the woods to observe the migration of some *Pyrrharctia isabella*. It looked as if the man with the gun had come back to park there and wait for Heather, or he was waiting for *me*, to lead me toward the end of my story.

I slowed down as I passed the truck, and there he was, the man with the gun, his body hunched over the steering wheel. He turned his head as I passed and our eyes met, I raised my hand or he raised his, I can't remember now, in recognition, and I carried on driving over the hill where Heather's house should, in principle, appear. I turned around at the crossroads, and when I came back the truck was driving toward the village. I followed it right to the other side of the mountain, then it turned into a lane leading to a house that was almost entirely hidden by trees.

There was just one name on the mailbox: H. W. Thorne. It chilled my blood to read this name, in red paint in the middle of a rectangle whose edges were fading. This name, Thorne, that I thought belonged only to Heather, detached itself from the black surface of the mailbox to mock me, or so it seemed, and remind me that the mysterious man who'd appeared in the woods the night I'd launched Heather's car into them was not acting solely according to his own will, but according to laws I didn't know since I hadn't decreed them myself.

Beyond the trees that hid H. W. Thorne's house, if that really was his name, a lamp had just been lit, and I noticed that dusk had fallen without my noticing. Disoriented by this sudden darkness, I knocked over a sign as I turned around — "No Hunting" — and I raced back home wondering if H. W. Thorne was Heather's father, brother, uncle, or husband, or if he was just a usurper. Sitting at my desk now, I wonder when I will go to visit him, and what attitude I will take with this man who has inserted himself, uninvited, between Heather and me.

Since yesterday, a third cat has been living with us, a little calico with multicoloured fur — beige, brown, white, and black — whom we encouraged to come inside to get her out of the cold. For now, she prefers it in the basement, where we've put a few blankets and a litter box. Our house is now a three-cat house, each one having its own floor. Now all we need is a fourth cat to live in the attic, so that at any time of day someone looking from the road would see a cat framed in one window of each storey.

It was near Lake Drolet, which I'll now call Two Hill Lake — "to give the landscape a voice," as P. says — that I kissed a boy for the first time and felt a red pulsing rise in my temples, then a dampness between my legs, filled with the scent of soft flesh, and a need to get away at all costs before my body toppled over on the wooden dock.

I've forgotten this boy's name, but not his face, his black eyes, so black, the warmth of his breath, or the slightly bitter scent teenage desire gives off, like a mixture of fresh, pink meat, and milk that's beginning to curdle. For months, the disturbing odour of lingering guilt emerging from this smell followed me, accompanied by a feeling I needed to expiate myself of a sin whose dizzying possibility I had barely anticipated.

A few decades later, I think about that boy every time I look at Two Hill Lake, its waters still giving off an aroma that my fear of vice and its consequences has transformed into a stench. I hate Two Hill Lake and turn my gaze away from the dark mass it makes at this time of day to look, instead, at H. W. Thorne's house. From the road, all I can see is the crescent of light hanging over the front door and the yellow glow of the ceiling pendant illuminating the glass squares of the door from the inside. One lamp in another room is also on, but the wide pine branches along the driveway that leads to the house mean that I can barely make it out.

I get out of the car, careful not to slam the door, and, because it's so dark that I can barely see three feet in front of my nose, I follow the ruts gouged into the snow by H. W. Thorne's truck up the driveway. Approaching the house, I crouch behind the low branches of a Virginia pine at a spot where I have a view of the entire property. Seen up close, H. W. Thorne's house looks like the kind of place you'd call inviting, the warmth emanating from it accentuated by its red shutters. But for all that, a powerful malaise grips me as I take in the paint flaking off the eavestroughs, the chimney smoking weakly, the dry trees along the porch. It's as if the house is hiding from some kind of imminent catastrophe.

For a moment I feel as though I've been transported into one of those movies in which the camera slowly zooms in on the place where drama is about to unfold and the music builds and heightens the tension though, because I am concentrating on the image, I don't notice it until the discordant crescendo that accompanies the hand, dagger, or bloody hammer shown to us in close-up to justify the scream accompanying the music. I hold my breath and look toward the lit window, where I can see H. W. Thorne sitting in an armchair behind which hangs, in a wooden frame, the photograph of a young woman whose features I can't quite make out but who seems familiar. I leave the cover of the Virginia pine, move closer to the house, and see it is actually a photograph of Heather, likely taken a few years ago. In the middle of the picture, Heather is laughing and pointing a gun at me.

The colour drains from my face and I suppress a gasp, which would, in a horror film, have filled the screen. I stand up and run to my car, not worrying about being unmasked. A few yards from the road I trip and fall prostrate in snow hardened by the red truck's tires. When I lift up my head, two feet are planted on the ground in front of me, shod in sturdy winter boots just like the ones the La Languette snowmobilers were wearing in the violent scene I'd imagined a few months before. I know the boots aren't real, that they only exist in the movie where the camera moves toward H. W. Thorne's house and pushes aside the branches as it goes, but this time I let out a cry.

When I get back to my car, I turn the heating on full blast and wait for the spasms in my right knee to stop before setting off again. The dark mass of Two Hill Lake is spread out at the foot of the mountain. I'll have to ask M.-J., who's been my friend since forever and always will be, what was the name of that boy with black eyes, because I know she kissed him too, before me, after me, whenever.

A pine grosbeak has just smashed into one of my study windows and is lying in the snow, wings half open, eyes set in black water. It's the second time this week that a grosbeak has knocked itself out on the window, perhaps confusing the weak light of my lamp with sunshine rising on a new spring. The first one survived, or at least it managed to take off again, but this one might die right here in the snow, simply for having believed in that non-existent sun.

This morning I hate winter, and I'm starting to hate this window of mine that kills birds, but through which blowing snow and wind still manage to enter and allow me to plan all possible worlds for Heather and H. W. Thorne.

Three days a week or more, I have to explain the same fucking rules. Aside from writing, it's what I do for a living: I edit.

I edit to pay the bills, I strike through, I insert, I rage, day in day out, never-ending, on days when, for purely financial reasons, I cannot write "Heather left the narrow clearing in which her car was stuck with the aim of finding some water. She found some not far off, at the bottom of a slope, a stream in which she is reflected but does not recognize herself. She says, 'My name is Heather Thorne,' but in the reflection the clear water returns, her lips are barely moving."

As the blowing snow dances among the tops of the trees, and the glacial wind lifts the wool scarf I've tied around my neck, I ask the night if my last days will follow this horizontal line, this path with neither bend nor slope that could be called the final straight before death. I contemplate the possibility that the hours before an announced or hoped-for death may never be so unwavering. I am aware that hours exist which relentlessly fold themselves back into the past, hours that coil up and cling on to any hint of life still remaining, and reject the terrifying perspective of an arrow striking the heart at this moment of our vanishing and heralding a collision, an explosion caused by our meeting a void absorbing the light caught on the shards of black glass lacerating the very fabric of thought.

Vertigo overwhelms me and I have to lean on the fence to catch my breath and distance myself from the concrete conception of the death I was on the point of bringing on, or so it seemed, leaving me feeling like those elderly people who simply decide, one day, that the road stops there; they've made it down the final straight and calmly dive into the scattering shards of black glass as they put their barely sipped cup of coffee back down on the table.

These dark thoughts make me feel nauseous in their turn. I try to shake it off, take a few steps toward the house on my tingling legs, and stop under the arch where Heather stood not long ago. The cat in my study watches me from the window. The second cat, slightly unbalanced on its three legs, looks out from a window on the second floor, and is staring at something invisible to my eye among the storm-frightened trees. And, in the dirty glass of the door leading to the basement, the aloof silhouette of the small calico cat appears like a cut-out, gazing at the blowing snow. To perfect this picture and stop the house from collapsing, I draw another cat spying out on the night from behind one of the dusty attic windowpanes, a grey cat with green eyes, whose yowling pulls me out of my trance.

Behind the first cat, there's a woman sitting at her desk. She motions at me to come in. A gust of wind blows my scarf and I take it off, the better to feel the soft fall on the other side of the arch, and join the woman, Heather, who needs me to untie the threads of this story I'm tangled up in, in which I don't know what role Gilles Ferland might play, and from which I should have expelled H. W. Thorne before he got too involved. But the dice have been cast, and the sheer fatigue I am experiencing at the very idea of retracing my steps far outweighs any exhaustion the presence of these two characters causes me. I'm getting old, it's true, and no longer have the courage to press the Delete key and write over my own palimpsests or trample in the shade of too many dying butterflies.

I open the door and sit down at the desk. Outside, my scarf is flapping around the arch in ghostly shapes reminding me that only death, only the absence of wind is able to eradicate our obsessions and lay them gently on the ground.

Winter is ending again. In two days it will be spring.

At dusk I saw two white swans in the branches of a spruce tree. People would say it was an illusion. People would say it was two heaps of snow. People would accuse me of dreaming. And I would answer them no, with my very own eyes I saw two white swans about to take off.

Today, it's murky out. I was waiting excitedly for the forecast big downpours, even if it meant bailing out the water that seeps into the basement every time the thaw gets under way, but all that's been falling since dawn is a little spitting rain that turns the landscape all grey and brown and will barely melt the snow in which I walk with difficulty, thinking how at this latitude the equinox is nothing more than another climatic lie, like those January suns accompanied by only biting cold.

To counter the effects of these lies on my low morale, I walk in paths that neither P. nor I could muster up the energy to dig out after the latest snow fell, trusting that the warmth would soon bring trickles that would become flows of slush, streams, muddy grass between the snowbanks, and that we'd be able to wade around in our rubber boots and get drunk on the smell of humus I associate with the joy I felt as a child when, in the evenings after school, I realized winter was over.

For now, I sink up to my knees in the leather boots I bought on sale at Canadian Tire in anticipation of the cold season, and huff and puff, nevertheless enjoying the almost warm wind blowing the branches, and the softness of the rain on my face, dripping down my neck and making me feel alive.

After a first trip, I cross the paths a second and then a third time, crushing the snow and opening up the path, growing wider and harder because of my repeated marching, happy to feel my thigh muscles contracting almost painfully with each new step, and the blood warming the cheeks I offer up to the fine rain. At the end of an hour of this labour, I collapse near a pine tree, my body too weary to carry me any further. The lenses of my glasses are covered in water droplets that, little by little, obscure the sky, and I stay there, a woman alive beneath the clouds.

Sitting on her old stump, Heather has started reading *Paterson*, and stops at this verse she does not understand:

Clearly, they say. Oh clearly! Clearly?
What more clear than that of all things
nothing is so unclear, between man and
his writing, as to which is the man and
which the thing and of them both which
is the more to be valued

———

I went back to visit V. in the mountains, telling myself it had to be impossible for him not to know H. W. Thorne since their houses are not far apart, and in such a remote area you always know your neighbours. He seemed surprised to see me back again, conscious, as I was, that old friends generally don't renew their ties in spite of the promises they exchange on the doorstep. "I've come about the man with the gun," I said, before even saying hello, and he asked me to come in.

The kitchen still smelled of fresh coffee, but V. offered me a beer instead and suggested we drink it on the patio out back in the sun. From there, the view was over the south side of the mountain, rather than Two Hill Lake. There was still a layer of compact snow under the trees, but around the patio there was a wide expanse of brown grass where a few little green shoots were starting to poke through. In two weeks, murmured V., as he pointed at the snow-covered undergrowth, all this will be forgotten. And then he reconsidered, well aware that whoever experiences snow like this every year cannot forget it—even at the height of summer, even when everything is in bloom. And really, that's what makes the summer so precious: the memory of the snow, the memory of it returning.

After we'd exhausted the subject of the temperature, V. offered me a second beer and asked me to tell him about the man with the gun. So I told him everything, starting with his meeting Heather after the accident and continuing on right up to the photo of Heather in his bedroom, or was it his office, but the further along I reached in my tale, the more strangely V. looked at me. We were finishing up our third beer when he admitted to understanding nothing about my story, and rephrased in his own words those H. W. Thorne had spoken: "Bev, the woman you're telling me about is not who you think she is . . ."

In the snowy undergrowth, the words reverberated like an echo from the shadows, *she's not who you think she is, Bev* . . . V. told me that Heather Waverley Thorne had died at the age of seventeen, some thirty-five years earlier. "If the woman you're telling me about is claiming to be called Heather—Heather Waverley Thorne—then she must be an imposter. But you know that as well as I do," he added, as the echo faded away in the spring air.

We'd been chatting for two hours, and a faint numbness swept through me as my hair stuck to my skull and an unpleasant layer of sweat covered my forehead. My first reaction was to burst out laughing. Where did this name Waverley come from, *Wave*, like the sea, like the ocean? And why had V. called me Bev, short for Beverley?

None of it made any sense. V. shouldn't have claimed that Heather was an imposter or that I was in league with her. And V. can't have forgotten who I am. The heat had confused me. The heat and the snow sparkling in the sun. Clearly, I'd lost the thread of the conversation and must have misinterpreted V.'s words when he'd told me about some young woman who was dead. It was that simple: I'd misunderstood, drunk too much alcohol, misheard, with the result that the names were all mixed up. I'd confused Heather with Esther, Waverley with Beverley, Beverley with Andrée.

I laughed again, a little hysterically perhaps, realizing V. didn't think I was funny at all. He was staring at my face as if he no longer recognized me, which was really and truly the case, and obviously found my fit of laughter somewhat out of place. So I stood up, slowly unfolding my tingling limbs, and headed to my car. In my rear-view mirror I could see V., puzzled by my drunkenness, getting smaller and smaller in the distance, and then, just before I turned off to take the road that cut the mountain in two, I saw him raise his hand in farewell or goodbye, his smile identical to Heather's in the picture hanging on the wall of H. W. Thorne's bedroom or office.

On my way back, trees swayed in the light, the mixed-up words pinged around in my head, and I couldn't understand what had just happened. Instead of going straight home I went to the 4th Line, where I walked up to the carcass of Heather's Buick, and a crow flew out of it. Heather wasn't there, but the trampled grass near the car indicated that she'd been there not too long before. As I approached, I noticed that since my last visit, the vegetation had grown up on the right side of the vehicle, blocking the passenger door and covering the axles.

Instead of abandoning myself to more nervous laughter, the intensity of which would render my face muscles tense again, I lay down on the swaying ground. The sky was shining through the branches and, half drunk, among the cawing crows, I no longer knew whether I was alive or not.

I didn't want P. to see me in this state.

A dog just passed by in the forest.

"Jackson!" Heather shouted.

Then the dog disappeared.

The second cat isn't doing well. The second cat is sleeping badly, his head resting on his bowl, as if he wants to absorb from the tinned salmon the memories of rivers where he fished. The second cat will die soon, and all we can hope for now is that he has a few more summer days remaining.

It's hard to write when you know someone in your house is going to die. It's hard not to get caught up in sadness and regrets, to resist the temptation to go sit under the pines, ass in the damp snow, bleating like a calf, a tiny little calf that will not have a chance to grow, that won't see the summer, that won't see the fall, that will barely see anything, dammit! It's hard not to think about the one who's about to depart, or about this miserable life we so want to render gentle, even if nothing can really mitigate the life of a creature from whose body violence and stupidity have chopped off a leg.

And how not to think of one's own death, about the stupidities one inflicts on oneself, day after day, all as idiotic as the day before, contemplating this time lost between two breaths of fresh air, two genuine moments of plenitude? I don't know how not to. I don't know how not to and I give up. I order myself to stop. I shout to myself that it's enough, shut up, this won't get you anywhere, so be quiet. Death will come regardless—death that might be a deliverance, but still I don't care. I don't want to be delivered from the wind. I don't want the second cat to be delivered from the summer we'd wanted him to enjoy.

So I imagine him limping on his three legs, breathing in the scent of the cedars, pausing by the wild roses, a happy cat in the June splendour. *Stop, for Christ's sake! Stop!* Shut your stupid mouth and write, smile at the cat, tell the cat you love him, write, write his name, Beauboule, then go back into the cold wind of the woods with Heather.

And the wind was cold. But the forest was deserted. "Heather!" I shouted at the top of my lungs. "Heather!" I shouted ten times, twenty, pulling at the ferns and brambles clinging to the side of the Buick with my bare hands amid the muted croaking of the crows complaining. And the day came to an end on my standing shadow.

Interlude. I wail. With my ass in the damp snow and my face to the sun.

The dark-eyed juncos are back, a sign that spring is no longer an illusion and only a few days of snow remain for our eyes to contemplate. I saw a junco yesterday, as my butt was getting damp, and thought *snow bird* to myself, because that's what my mother used to call the juncos that heralded the final snowfalls. I also saw flies mating on the doorframe, a few more shoots of green grass coming up in the big brown stretches we'll soon have to clean up. And I heard a mourning dove close by, cooing its love song that sounds like the loon's lament. Today, April 13, the mercury will hit 19 degrees.

Beauboule is resting. He looks almost serene. The calico is purring at my feet, and the first cat is chasing field mice and voles behind the house. I wonder whether V., when we were chatting on his patio with beers in hand, really did call me Bev. I try to remember our conversation, his reaction to the story I was telling him, and then those words he could have taken straight from H. W. Thorne: *The woman you're telling me about is not who you think she is*. Which was when, if I'm not mistaken in my reconstruction of that warm, sunny afternoon, V. called me Bev. *Bev, the woman you're telling me about is not who you think she is.* Those were his exact words, their echo then ringing out in the shadows of the undergrowth: *Bev . . . not who you think she is . . .*

I tried to remember further back, to remember if, at any other point in our conversation, he'd called me by some other name—Andrée, Andrée A., or even Heather. I replayed our chat on a loop, but did not hear V. say my name. All I could hear was *Bev*, and I understood that V. really was confusing me with Beverley, a girl with brown hair and around my height who used to be part of our group. I realized V. must have thought I was Beverley, the brown-haired girl who lived at the top of the tall hill. He thought I was Beverley Simons, and that I'd lost weight over time.

I looked at myself in the mirror and noticed that in truth, after all these years, it would be possible for someone to take me for Bev, who also had a narrow nose and blue eyes. "My name's Beverley," I said to the reflection I was staring at, "Bev to my friends, but you can call me Andrée, Andrée A.," and I let the tears flow that I'd been holding back for so long, a few bitter tears from Beverley's blue eyes.

Night has fallen. The first cat has come in and is sleeping on his armchair. All is right with the world, or at least with the usual order of things, but tonight I can't seem to find my place at the heart of this orderliness which usually guarantees my equilibrium. I haven't stopped thinking about V. all day, about his too-close resemblance (apart from his wrinkles) to the young man he used to be, and I wonder if V. really is V., or if I'm getting things mixed up by thinking he's V. when really he's T. or D. or L.

I also think about that name, Waverley, which, apart from the shushing sound of waves, doesn't bring anything specific to mind. Waverley, whose first letter matches the second initial marked on H. W. Thorne's mailbox. What if there is no H. W. Thorne other than Heather Waverley, and the man with the gun is still waiting to be named?

I line up the first and last names of my characters, each one more elusive than the last, and try out various permutations, a few slight modifications, until my bedroom walls start to move like waves and a powerful feeling of nausea sees me rush to the bathroom, where I vomit up bile in front of photos of Walt Whitman and Stephen King.

Once I'm back in my bed, I tell myself that maybe V. is called D. or T. or even L. for liar, D. for dissembler, T. for trickster, because it's obvious V. knows more than he wants to admit, more than he's ready to tell me. I put my head down on the pillow and sleep on these questions: Who is V.? Who is V. and what does he want from me?

It's a time of death. When I opened my bedroom curtains this morning, I saw a body stretched out on the ground right outside my house. The cat, I thought for a devastating fraction of a second, racing in my pyjamas down the stairs and outside. Even though I knew the body lying on the road wasn't the cat's, I ran through the mud, fuck the slippers, right up to the lifeless body, so my fear could understand that what my eyes were telling me was true: the sight of the body that had made my heart pound in my chest for a brief but intense moment of pain was real, but the body out there was not my cat's.

On the damp asphalt lay either Alberte or Albertine, one of the female raccoons that come every night, spring and autumn, to empty the bird feeders with their gaggle of lesser Alberts, Albertes, and Albertines. I moved a few steps closer and recognized Alberte, big bloody Alberte, whom I could not mistake for any of the little Albertes because of her size. I examined the animal's stomach, in which there was no longer any breath, and then murmured, "Dammit, Alberte, what were you thinking? You know they drive like maniacs along here." Then I cursed the vehicles that pile the carcasses up at the sides of the roads, whether summer, spring, fall, or winter, though fuck it, it's in spring first of all — spring above all — that they take away the animals' mortal winds.

I looked at Alberte's tail one final time, a horizontally striped tail, not like the cat's tail at all, and went back inside, my heart broken by the thought of Alberte mown down in the middle of the night, of Alberte, whom I'd assumed, for a brief but intensely painful moment, was the cat watching the birds from the section of the fence that disappears into the cedars.

When P. looked at me quizzically, I said, "Alberte is dead, I'm going to go get her." But P. told me not to worry, my slippers were all dirty and he'd take care of it. There was nothing else to say. He put on his shoes and went out to pick up the body and move it to the ditch, because we don't leave an animal's body in the middle of a road where it will be run over by sixty wheels every hour. P. was wearing his work gloves and picked Alberte up with the respect due to every living thing living no longer, and we didn't say another word about it, or barely, because every attempt to discuss the event of a death, and not *the* death that will one day happen, can only exacerbate the intensity of the desiccated feeling already devastating us. We didn't want to be gloomy, our spirits weighed down by *death*, such a heavy word, for the rest of the day. But there, we know, is Alberte in the ditch, dead and already decomposing.

I try to shed a bit of light on Heather's middle name and end up concluding that Waverley is the thing about Heather I'll never figure out, an unknowable part of a character only accessible to the author through other characters. Waverley proves to me that I've not invented everything, after all.

When I parked in V.'s driveway, his car wasn't there. I knocked on the door just in case, but there was no answer. Not knowing how long he would be, I decided to wait for him on the patio at the back, the sun still beating down. Strangely, V. hadn't tidied away our glasses, nor the bottles we'd emptied and the ashtray we'd filled, as if he'd gone away in a hurry immediately after I'd left two days earlier. There was a little bit of beer in one of the glasses on the table, which I swallowed in one go, even though I was expecting it to be warm. The beer was still cold, not flat, and it didn't have the bland taste of drinks left out. Which meant that V. must have gone out just a few minutes ago, soon after getting himself the beer he'd not finished.

The mess on the table reminded me of how drunk I'd been the day before yesterday. I pulled a chair into the shade at the edge of the wood and sat listening to the chirping juncos that had gathered there as well. The snow had receded further into the undergrowth, revealing ground strewn with broken branches, pine needles, dry fluff, and brown spotted leaves. I looked at my hands, which were also spotted, and bent down to gather a pile of leaves soaked in the damp soil and applied them to my hands. You never know what mixture might miraculously return your youth to you, that's what I was thinking at that moment—there had to be a herb somewhere, a plant whose essence had the power to soften age spots, or some water so cool it would grasp the skin and take away its endless tiredness. Then I took off my shoes and started paddling in a pool of melted snow.

It was just starting to rain when I decided to leave, my hands and feet covered in the spring mud Heather had put all over her body back there, near the stream flowing over the moss, either to camouflage herself or because she was losing her mind. Probably for both of those reasons. That's what happens when you're alone. That's what happens when you're afraid. You hide away and start imagining stories, each one more real than the last.

Right now, Heather is telling herself a guerrilla story in which each tree is hiding a bearded man pointing an object made of metal and wood at her. A gun, she thinks, as she takes advantage of the rain that's also pouring down on the 4th Line and covering the sound of her advance to crawl through the wet leaves to the bank where her Buick is.

When she reaches the bank, her hands scraped by the rock, she hides behind the car to examine the cuts bleeding pink blood diluted by the rain. Wondering about the realness of this blood, she turns back to the forest and whispers to a woman as real as her stories, "Tell me I'm not going crazy, tell me this is going to stop." And I don't know how to reply to her, because I too am moving forward, barefoot on uneven ground.

To get home, I walked along the stream to Castonguay, so-called after a man who died nearly two centuries ago but who left his mark in the place names here, probably because, before either the route or the village existed, he built himself a cabin at the stream's source. The hill where I live was, at the time, virgin land that the Castonguays, the Paradis, the Royers, the Saint-Pierres and others had hacked away at with axes and chilblains. I needed to remember that, to remember that the world hasn't always been the way it is, won't always have the astonishing beauty bestowed on it by the rain near the stream.

To fix these pictures in my mind, I stopped by the little waterfall that feeds into the northeast tip of Raspberry Tree Lake. I went down into the ditch to inhale the moisture and removed a piece of the stratified rock constricting the flow of the river in this place, a beautiful sharp stone with which I traced an H for Heather in my left palm, joined to the inverted W for Waverley made by my lifelines — my death lines, my fortune lines, my destiny lines. Then I traced another H at the bend of my right wrist, above the M or the W, depending on which way you read it, that is already there. This letter will represent the mark of the stream, the mark of the past that must not be forgotten.

When I plunged my hands into the cold water, a thin trickle of blood was carried by the current, dissolving in the foamy whirlpool eroding the first river bend. Two Canada geese took flight from the lake above us, Heather and Waverley, descendants of the long line of geese that return every year to this spot. I let out a goose cry to greet them, and they disappeared in the colours of the sky, like those proud birds of Riopelle's.

Afterwards I walked some more, finally arriving at my house soaked from head to toe and with an almost invisible bloodstain where I'd wiped my hand on my pants, but feeling every bit as content as if the gates of paradise had been opened to me. I thanked the rainy sky and went back to work.

A trail of damp tracks marked the path from the kitchen to my study, where I lit the lamp whose weak glow once again cleaved the cat's body in two. I took off my shirt and pulled an old wool sweater on over the t-shirt I wanted to keep on in order to write with the rain imprinted on my body. As I wait for Heather to appear I draw a wrecked Buick being eaten away by rust. I sketch out the skeletal silhouette of a few leafless trees and see Heather crawl around the car on her elbows, breathing haltingly and glancing behind her to let me know that she thinks someone is there.

She crouches down by the driver's door and manages to open it with her outstretched right arm, then slips quickly into the vehicle. She grabs the axe lying on the back seat and looks to the setting sun as she wipes her face, the mud already starting to dry. She waits for a few long minutes during which nobody comes, and then she rummages frantically in the glove compartment. After a few seconds she finds what it is she's looking for, an old lead pencil and an ad for motor oil. On the back of the ad she writes, "The first is called Ferland and the second McMillan."

Then she puts the note in an obvious position on the dashboard, grabs the axe, and gets out of the car. She hides behind the pile of branches she'd stacked up at the edge of the clearing, anticipating brutal cold, and, holding the axe in front of her, waits for Ferland and McMillan's shadows to stand out in the moonlight.

The first is called Ferland and the second McMillan. I read this phrase again by the flashlight Heather left in her car and consider, again, how angry Gilles Ferland had been when, just before Christmas, he'd ordered me off his property, and I think about the words I myself put in the mouth of one of the two men in La Languette, *Gilles, fuck, tell me we didn't just do that.* Behind the branches, Heather looks nervously at the path that her daily comings and goings have created.

The cat is running like a crazy horse from one end of our property to the other, his fur pressed down against his sleek body by the wind rushing past him; his fur like the white manes whipping against the muscular necks of animals rendered wild by a taste of the plains. The cat is running like a crazy horse and the cat is happy. The cat, *mon amour.*

In his book *Zen and the Art of Motorcycle Maintenance,* Robert M. Pirsig writes:

> Lateral knowledge is knowledge that's from a wholly unexpected direction, from a direction that's not even understood as a direction until the knowledge forces itself upon one. Lateral truths point to the falseness of axioms and postulates underlying one's existing system of getting at truth.

This is the direction I must follow, under the aegis of the trails and lateral knowledge we typically apprehend only out of the corner of our eye, that get lost in the periphery of our gaze and muddled as soon as we turn our heads, erasing the detail that we only half perceived, vague signs whose meaning we might have understood had we not insisted on following the pointers left by those who walked straight ahead.

I have to leave the path again and again, stepping over holes, stumbling on sharp stones and falling into side pits full of rubbish, corpses, obstacles, and truths too raw to be offered up to the sight of anyone who cannot bear death's omnipresence.

Still hiding behind the heap of branches, Heather can distinguish more shadows the moonlight has not washed out, among them the silhouettes of two drunk men, one of them very tall — Ferland — and looking even more so as the moon seems to stretch his body unsteadily over the whole forest. The other one is shorter and stockier and belongs to McMillan, whose thick red hair is reminiscent of the shining fur of a fox, and whose shadow begins to start like a yelping beast backed into a corner, while the taller one's arms move forward, snaking between the branches, *Come on, baby, we aren't gonna hurt you*, and then an axe falls down on the snaking arms and on the piled-up branches, sending a few chunks of bark flying, *Let me go, you fuckers, get off me!* Then a nervous fox backed into a corner appears in front of Heather's panicked eyes, who strikes, dammit, and strikes and strikes the shadows the moon has flattened on the ground near her shining axe blade.

I pulled on my rubber boots and left the road to walk in the ditch, along the stream of scattered coltsfoot, little yellow flowers that bloom even before the snow has completely melted. Today, however, there is no more snow in the ditch, nor in the fields, nor in the undergrowth. All that remain at sparse intervals are a few hardened patches covered with sand, gravel, and all the black winter residues that block the sun's rays and stop iced matter from turning into brown water.

I push this residue aside with my feet, lift up a few stones, and pull up some roots without meaning to, discovering as I go a plastic bottle stuck in the sludge, a page from a newspaper reporting on some violent act I'd rather not know about, and a cartridge from a buckshot implicated in another violent act. I pick up the shell, imagining that it might still smell of fire, lead, powder, and, in fact, it does give off a gun-like burnt metal smell — unless I've dredged that particular scent up from some memory of the hot summer when my father was teaching me how to shoot wooden targets. I associate this memory with the photograph of Heather brandishing a gun, and recall the note she scribbled in a rush before wrestling with the shadows attacking her: *The first is called Ferland and the second McMillan.*

I examine the shiny cartridge and decide Ferland and McMillan must have come this way, that these men are everywhere beyond the road's unnaturally flat surface that the mundane barbarity of idiocy occurs. I put the cartridge in my pocket and follow the winding stream home. It is bordered here and there by cattails, their fluff sticking to my clothes. In front of the house, behind the guardrail at the edge of a slight drop in the ground, Alberte's dismembered body sinks into the coltsfoot.

William Carlos Williams is taunting me from the pages of *Paterson*, challenging me to carry on reading. I feel as if I'm never going to finish the book, as if *Paterson* is rejecting me, or that I might penetrate its opaqueness only to find myself suddenly standing in front of a void. I can't stand seeing *Paterson* on top of my pile of half-read books, so I pick it up and leaf through it, stopping at the place on page 193 where another reader — Heather, I assume, or P. — has underlined a sentence warning me about authors influencing their characters: "Norman Douglas (*South Wind*) said to me, The best thing a man can do for his son, when he is born, is to die."

I read the sentence again and can no more understand its meaning than figure out why Williams chose to cite this fragment of conversation with Douglas. To provoke readers, of course, and force them to ask whether the father, the mother, the creator, should hide themselves behind what they've put into the world, even at the risk of suffocating, castrating, or erasing it. Williams wants to tease us, as did Douglas, imbued with sufficient self-regard to deem the father's death necessary.

Sensing the advent of one of those brutal headaches that distort the words lined up on the page, I close the book and curse Williams, disinclined to share whatever was his point of view regarding sentences he's throwing our way—and, naturally, I curse Douglas too, because he surely had no children, and only a father who had no interest in committing suicide before little Norman was born.

I remain preoccupied by the subtext of Douglas's affirmation: is it time for me to die and entrust the entirety of the story to Heather? I'm tempted to ask P., who's reading quietly in the living room, but I know it's too much to ask someone else to pronounce on my and Heather's possible deaths, and even more because her world is its own, and any outside interaction might start tremors that could destabilize the ground on which Heather and I are coming into being.

It's up to me to decide if my presence in Heather's life is in fact necessary, and, too, if the loss of the father could in some absurd way be beneficial to the orphan.

I put *Paterson* down on the black table and tell P. I'm leaving for the mountain and don't know when I'll be back.

Since my last visit to H. W. Thorne the trees had closed in over the drive leading to his house—all I could see of the road is grey—and so I set off with a certain amount of apprehension.

There was no sound other than that of my feet on the gravel, not even a bird or two singing. A dark, cloudy, threatening mass had settled over the mountain, spreading its shade right over to the other slope. As I looked around, I'd had the impression the place was dead, or was pushing the living away, a sensation belied by the flight of a partridge, the noise of its flapping wings almost overwhelming me. The sound of my heart reverberating in my temples melded with the crunching of the gravel and I'd stopped for a moment to regain my composure. "Calm down, Michaud, it was just a startled bird," but these words I'd been repeating to myself for years when I needed to contain my anger or reduce my fear and anxiety, *Calm down, Michaud*, don't have the desired effect. Something was not quite right, as if nobody had lived here for a long time, even though I'd seen the man with the gun in the winter, and the ruts dug by his truck's wheels were still fresh.

In front of the house, however, there was no truck, and H. W. Thorne must then have been absent. My determination started to waver, but I decided to wait a while, hoping I'd have more success with him than I'd had with V.

I approached hesitantly, aware that I'd be violating a place whose welcome had so far been refused me. I also feared making H. W. Thorne angry if he found me sitting quietly on his porch upon his return, or strolling around the weed-infested garden. Nonetheless I made the circuit of the house, just in case the truck was parked out of sight.

Behind the house was a large wooden deck like V.'s, facing the forest. On the patio, two chairs were set around a low table on which I thought I could see some glasses and a few bottles of beer. V. wasn't the only person to have added on a deck, but I was struck by its design, the smallest detail of which, right down to the ashtray overflowing with cigarette butts, matched my memory of V.'s deck exactly. Were I to advance across the few metres separating me from the low table, I was convinced I'd find in one of the abandoned glasses a few sips of beer indicating H. W. Thorne had only just left. This certainty didn't just come from the similarity between the places, but also because, I suddenly realized with biting lucidity, I was the one who'd constructed this set and poured the beer now sitting at the bottom of one of the glasses.

I let myself slide against the bannister, its handrail as solid as any other, and sat down on the ground, one buttock on a flat stone and the other one at an angle, arms resting on my knees and my gaze lost in the undergrowth where the snow had recently melted. But I was so over-whelmed that I no longer knew if spring had actually arrived or if I'd sat in a snowbank, the existence of which I needed to deny at any cost, though without which the very reference points on which my own existence relied would disappear.

I closed my eyes and touched the ground to make sure it wasn't cold as snow, and forced myself to crawl on all fours—to smell the new earth, the dry hay, the little tufts of young grass poking up here and there. Then I touched, turned over and smelled the earth until I could be cer-tain that I wasn't wrong about the course of the seasons. The earth was real and so was its damp coolness; the hay smelled of hay, and the mud stuck under my short finger-nails. But the deck adjoining H. W. Thorne's house hid a truth that I didn't dare admit: I was responsible for V. and H. W. Thorne having to leave their houses simply because I'd refused to learn who Heather Waverley Thorne was, and—if what V. had told me was true—what the cir-cumstances of her death were some thirty-five years earlier, according to V., and why she'd come back to haunt me.

I stood up and brushed off my clothes. I looked at H. W. Thorne's house and wondered if it was real—if H. W. Thorne had ever existed, and if V., my childhood friend whom I'd not seen in thirty years, was just the product of my imagination.

Some mirrors seem to want to reflect the world in its entirety but only send back light in order to magnify the contours of the beings gazing at their reflection. And some are closed mirrors, like the calm waters that slowly obscure the ovals of faces desperate for shade. Heather and I look at ourselves in one such mirror and add a touch of grey to our eyelids, just enough to weigh them down and for us to gently nod off, succumbing to sleep carried in by wispy winds of oblivion.

It's May 11. In three days my father will have been dead for forty-seven years. In the red-brick garage adjoining my family home, his old blue Buick Electra continues to disintegrate. All I have to do is think of it, and I'm on a summer road trip, feeling the wind whipping at my temples.

I'm nine years old and life is good. The warm water in the distance laps at the sand where I'm about to go and run around in my blue swimsuit with white polka dots. It's summer 1967. The summer of love. Kawasaki 750s and tanned girls with their hair flapping as the freedom-scented air roars past. On the radio, the hits play one after another and make the tanned girls dance without cares. The Buick is a Batmobile barrelling toward the horizon to take on bad guys, a racing car nothing can stop. My astonished eyes take in the endless back roads where I'll learn to read and write, my hair blowing in the wind as I cling to the shoulders of a man who will soon die, but who is firmly holding on to the steering wheel of the Batmobile and whistling an old Maurice Chevalier tune.

——

This morning, as I was filling the bird feeders, I said to myself that V. was one of those unexpected arrivals whose authenticity—and honesty—I needed to determine. If V. is lying, it must mean that V. is real, as it's unthinkable that I'd have created a character whose only purpose was to lie to me. What would become of truth then?

So the important thing is not to discover whether V. actually exists, but to determine whether what he says is true. If he's lying to me about Heather's death, then he's real. But if, on the other hand, he's telling the truth, that means I'm writing a story that other people are inventing along with me—and it's possible that I only exist because of these others. In both cases, V. exists, and the theory I'm trying to construct about the truthfulness or otherwise of V.'s words doesn't hold up. V. is as alive as Heather is.

The calico cat follows the path of my pen on the rough draft and tries to catch it each time I move to the next line, as if she wants to interrupt the backward movement that is crucial to the next sentence's momentum. Is the cat trying, by biting the pen's black plastic case, to stop me from uncovering the corpses strewn across my study in the bombyx's wake, spreading their rotten odour over the much-anticipated summer? I stare into the cat's green eyes and let my pen drop, but as soon as the object has stopped moving it no longer interests her.

I've started asking questions everywhere about a young woman named Heather Waverley Thorne, who would have lived in this area a few decades ago. First off, I interrogated the owner of the convenience store, where the gossip about everyone in the area circulates on a daily basis, but since she's only lived in the village for twenty years, she's not heard anything about a girl by that name, alive or dead.

I had no better luck at the hardware store, where all the employees were too young to know of any event linked to this hypothetical Heather Thorne. "Heather? Heather Waverley, you said? No, never heard of her."

The realization that half the village's inhabitants were young enough to be my children and would therefore have no memory of my own childhood years left me feeling terribly old. I was living in a world in which the ghosts and the dead outnumbered the living, in which the people with whom I might have talked about Gosselin Lake, the big rock, the old wooden college built in the shadow of the church, or the Texaco garage fire that kept the village population awake until dawn in July '64 or '65 were becoming rarer and rarer.

As I left the hardware store the sun beat down on me like a hammer on an anvil and I wanted to be crushed right there on the deck, waiting for the maggots to come and gnaw away at my body. But instead, I headed to the cemetery just next to it, in the hope of finding Heather Waverley Thorne's grave.

Heather wasn't likely to make a run for it, so first I paid homage to my father, as well as the trees around his tombstone, as if, were something from this man still living, it would exist now in the tree sap, and then in the buds that would imminently bloom. I said, "Hi Dad, hi trees," and waited, stiff as a board, in front of his grave, for his spirit, travelling among the trees, to respond to the tears that spring to my eyes every time I stand in this spot.

A gentle wind made the lowest branches move. I murmured, "Thanks, Dad, I love you, Dad," before walking, with my nose full of snot, over to the verdant plots where my other dead lay: Joseph, Élise, another Joseph, Angélina, Alcide, Gracia, Berthe, Suzanne, Lucien, Antonio, Béland, Cécile, Lorenzo, as well as women and children who'd died young and whom I'd never known but had one or the other of my two surnames — Audet and Michaud.

After extricating an old tissue from the bottom of my pocket, I started surveying the cemetery in minute detail, intent on discovering a gravestone with Heather's first and middle name — but also Thorne, the surname that had recently become my own — chiselled into it. I walked around the whole graveyard twice, from north to south and then east to west, I was even brazen enough to pull away with my bare hands some of the vegetation that had grown over stones lying on the ground, aware that I was engaging in a sort of profanity I'd have to explain were I caught in the act, but the urge was stronger than I was, and I needed to reassure myself that Heather had never been buried in this rectangle of either greenery or snow, depending on the season, visible from my childhood bedroom window.

I left the cemetery at dusk, my nails black, my knees grass-stained, but certain that Heather Thorne was alive, that V. had lied to me and, consequently, that he was not one of my creations.

The man with the gun has just parked his truck in the yard. From the kitchen I see H. W. Thorne. His two hands are on the steering wheel, and he seems to be hesitating over getting out of his vehicle and coming to meet me. The motor is still running, and I expect him to drive off again at top speed, sending gravel flying.

P. has just come down and said a man is parked outside the house. I tell him it's the man with the gun, and I've been expecting his visit. P. is quiet for a few moments, then asks me to send this stranger back where he came from, this man I've talked about on several occasions while conceding to P. that my universe is slipping away from me. According to P., nothing good will arise out of my meeting this "man who's come from elsewhere," as he's named him, emphasizing the fact that I have no hold over a character born of some blind spot in my story. Only it's impossible for me to send H. W. Thorne away, because now he's standing under the arch, between fall and spring.

When the light of the lamp illuminates just half of his face, the man with the gun vaguely resembles Heather, but I don't fall for the trick of the light and I wait for him to speak to me. Right now, he's talking about *Paterson*, which he saw on my desk, and he's alluded to the death of Sarah Cumming, Hopper Cumming's wife, who fell from the top of the Passaic River Falls on June 20, 1812, around two months after their wedding. He admits that this is more or less all he can remember about *Paterson*, this random fact narrated by Williams, about a slender woman toppling over in the mist, her veil grabbed by the tumultuous waters.

That's how he imagines Sarah Cumming—in a young bride's dress, her long brown hair slicked against the wet satin enveloping her cries, arms and legs flailing in a confusion of hair and fabric, and the chaotic folds of her dress revealing a glimpse of her immaculate underwear. According to him, there is nothing more shocking than the deaths in full flight of youth lost to a moment of distraction: one second of inattention and the foot slips, the eyes widen in the face of the inevitable, and it's all over. Two or three heartbeats and you are no more.

"It's all over," he repeats, "end of story, no more can be added, nothing." And then he leans toward me, his face now three-quarters lit by the lamp, and asks, "Why, then, why resuscitate the dead?"

How can I explain to him that Heather's return is not a resurrection at all, that a writer—even if she can, for just a few pages, resuscitate people whose absence is unbearable—cannot bring a woman back to life when she knows nothing of her death. I lean toward him in turn, our faces sharing the shadow, and murmur, "You're wrong. This woman, Heather, is not who you think she is, I haven't resuscitated anyone."

I'd hoped the man with the gun would seize the pole

I was holding out to him and reveal Heather Waverley Thorne's identity, but he retreated into such a silence that the wind coming in through the half-open window had Holy Crappy Owl spinning at the end of his rope. Suddenly interested in Crappy, H. W. Thorne wanted to know where the owl had come from.

"From another story," I answered. "He managed to get out of that one and slip into this one. Everyone comes from some story. So do you, but I have no idea which one."

I hadn't even finished my sentence before H. W. Thorne's expression turned surly and a wave of anger infused his face. He rose suddenly, picked up the first thing that came to hand and sent it flying against the wall, murmuring, in a tone unsettling Crappy, that he came from the same story as me, from the same story as Heather, from the same story as Sarah Cumming, whose departed body now accompanied our own. Then he snatched up his coat, a part of which brushed my face, and I smelled cedar, that fresh scent of the forest which had struck Heather so. In the heat of the moment I almost touched the man with the gun to reassure myself he was real but, in the face of his mounting anger, all the magic had flown away.

I stood up and tried to stop him leaving, but he was already through the door and disappearing into the cold night air. I watched as the rear lights of his truck disappeared behind the trees and sank into my armchair, the forest smell of his clothes still lingering. H. W. Thorne had just proved to me my inability to solve the mystery I had created. Without beating around the bush, he'd shown that I understood nothing; ever since I'd met Heather I'd been swimming in total darkness.

The rain started after H. W. Thorne left, and for three days we listened to its incessant rattling on the porch roof. "These are the great May seas," my mother would say, and, before her, my grandmother, one of whose ancestors no doubt came from one of those foggy places where May tides are affected by the clouds. The expression followed the ancestor, from beside the sea to beside the river, and ended up here at the foot of mountains that have never tasted a single drop of salt water.

I reminded my mother of the expression yesterday, when I visited her in the hospital where she's staying for a few months following a bad fall. I sat at the foot of her bed and talked to her about the great seas and ocean sprays she had conveyed to me, while in the room across the corridor a drama was playing out as it did every day, no less upsetting for that. I could hear cries coming out of the room, inconsolable cries, the kind that make you want to take the crying person in your arms and lead them away from the dying person.

Because this was exactly the kind of drama unfolding in the room opposite: someone was dying, no doubt a mother, a woman who also had numerous friends, and numerous siblings, whom I noticed as they filed into her room, one after another, twenty or so people with serious faces, coming to say their goodbyes and then gathering in the little lounge at the end of the corridor, from which an occasional peal of laughter would burst out, because you must face death however you can, and not let it seize you so tightly that it suffocates the laughter freeing you from it for a few moments.

I'd have preferred not to witness the spectacle, but right there, sitting at the foot of my mother's bed, it was impossible not to speculate about the movements of the silhouettes leaving and entering the dying woman's room, where they stayed for a short or long time depending on just how close they were to her, or on their ability to cope with the disarmingly bright eyes of the woman in the bed. All I could see were her legs, wrapped in a blue blanket that reminded me of a shroud, and whose stillness indicated to me that life was slowly leaving the body over which friends and relatives were bending for a last kiss.

I was unable to endure the intimacy of someone else's grief any longer, and pretended that I wanted to go out for a smoke in order to take refuge in the hospital's parking lot, where sunlight had finally pierced the clouds and was warming up the asphalt and the cars. I paced up and down some distance away from the Emergency entrance and thought about the dying woman, whose name and age I didn't know, wondering what you might feel when twenty faces came to remind you that you wouldn't be there tomorrow and would no longer be able to cherish these hands stroking your own.

Was this how I'd like to die? Surrounded by my people even as I was aware their very presence meant I was about to leave? Would I want to say my goodbyes in such heartbreak? Goodbyes to a world whose textures and winds I have so loved? The answer was no, and I decided not to dwell on the subject.

I stubbed out my second cigarette without worrying about all the butts I'd left behind in filthy ashtrays, then picked up a small, smooth stone I'd been examining for a few moments. It had the shape of a druid's hood, the sort of hat worn by magicians in illuminated manuscripts of the Middle Ages. I stroked its corners and slipped it into my coat pocket since it was, I knew, one of those stones from which a weary spirit can draw powers to repel death.

My mother is not well. P. is not well. The second cat is not well. I have to go outside.

Nobody's been through the clearing where Heather's Buick has been parked since the accident. As the days have passed, Heather has come to realize that nobody comes through the clearing for the simple reason that she is currently outside the world, and anyone who does venture this way finds themselves expelled from the dimension of ordinary people, a prisoner of the endless autumn, the yellowing trees, the damp nights accentuating the smell of decay that follows her wherever she goes.

Only the man with the gun has set foot on this bit of land, and he too is a prisoner of this interminable season — unless he's found a gap, an exit through which he has managed to break free from the stasis. But if not, he must still be there, and close by, waiting for the weather to clear and the snow to finally fall on the forest.

Heather also wonders what is beyond the forest, perhaps a desert, a paved road, or the sea. Then a falling leaf makes her jump and she sees Ferland and McMillan's faces again, the men whose names she's written down so they won't be forgotten, and the truth appears to her in its desperate bareness: beyond this forest there's another forest, and another, and another still, ravaged by a storm that is also infinite.

The second cat—write his name: "Beauboule, Beauboule the Magnificent, Beauboule the Admirable, Beauboule the Magnificent and Adorable"—the second cat dies on Friday and the house tilts dangerously.

The Tilted House. This is what I wanted to call my next novel, once I've put the final touches on my most recent one. The novel would have been about the fence that needs putting back up, the hill our house stands on, the wild roses growing on both sides of the land year after year, and I would have told no other story than that of the house, of the relationship between it and its inhabitants, of P. and the cats, of me and P. and so on. Like in a movie where nothing happens but the constant rigour of days, during which we need to fix the fence, feed the birds, paint the porch, pour wine for dinner.

I would have talked about that in the book as well, about the long conversations we have over a glass of wine, discussing, depending on our mood, the fence that has to be fixed, the latest news, asking did you know this, did you see that, and about the house being built a little further down the road, the brown one with black shutters, and about the springtime ladybug invasion, the insects appearing out of the tiniest cracks as soon as the sun has passed the equinox, all these subjects inevitably leading to what we are reading, to the novels I consume with varying degrees of enthusiasm, so dull and insipid are the times, and to P.'s readings about matter, about the constant movement of things, leading us in turn to talk about the wood of the table our wine is standing on.

I'd have taken on these subjects if it hadn't been for my walk on the 4th Line, which might have ended differently if I'd decided simply to go buy the newspaper or go and visit my old friend V. who lives on the mountain, in which case I'd have known nothing of Heather had I not met the woman earlier and experienced the ineluctable revelation of our having the same name.

Despite its title, *The Tilted House* would not have been a novel about imminent catastrophe, because catastrophe is always imminent. I'm thinking, among other things, of death, of the second cat, Beauboule. (Write his name.) No, it would have been a novel about the precariousness of what leans and needs to be propped up if you want it to remain standing; in summary, a novel about the angles that result from our desire to stabilize the inevitable collapse of our existence.

It would also have been about stories I might have written — this story, for instance, begun on the road to La Languette, explaining how two men, in the throes of a sudden madness, were in some way under a spell, were, in other words, victims of that other victim always referred to as "beauty," and that has always, since the dawn of time, caused a sudden craziness to germinate in people's minds — the futile desire to possess, destroy, or annihilate what can't be seized.

Before we took him to the place where skin, fur, eyes, and blood are reduced, no matter the colour of the coat, to white and grey ashes (let's not think about it too much), I needed to see and touch the second cat's corpse one last time: Beauboule, write his name, and write it again — "Beauboule" — to ensure that he, like Schrödinger's cat in a box, isn't condemned to exist for all eternity in a quantum purgatory where he is both alive and dead at the same time.

I flipped through the few notes I'd taken after that walk in La Languette when two men appeared to me at the start of the logging road that runs alongside the river, two men who were about to go crazy, and would go crazy again each time a quiet moment brought incendiary images of their nightmare back to them, images of those few unreal minutes during which, obliviously, they'd been possessed by a violence they'd thought themselves incapable of, by a rage shot through with red flashes of light, of blinding desires that would launch them into the abyss of those who know they are irremediably guilty.

On the third page of the Blueline notebook I used to jot down any ideas and thoughts relating to the novel that might have been called *Fall Day*, my notes ended with these words: "The first will be called Ferland and the second McMillan."

Under the carpet of the trunk of her car, where the spare wheel should have been, Heather found a gun engraved with her initials, H. W. T., and two boxes of bullets put there in case of danger. She doesn't know what the W stands for—her father's name, maybe; that face she remembers vaguely, its features blurring when she exposes them to too much light—but she is sure the gun belongs to him. After she's checked that it actually works, she practises by shooting one of the Buick's doors, where three almost straight rows of holes are now lined up.

This isn't the first time Heather Thorne has held a gun in her hands. As soon as she grips the weapon, the smell of powder returns to her memory, and she remembers how to support its wooden butt on her shoulder to absorb some of the recoil, and remembers, too, how the breech slides when you eject a cartridge. She squeezes the trigger a final time and closes her eyes until the echoes of the shot die away. The men called Ferland and McMillan can now arrive.

At dinner, P. talked to me once again about the philosophical trend he's interested in at the moment, a new materialism that some call *object-oriented ontology*, "Oh Oh Oh," for those in the know, perhaps hearing in the acronym the legendary laugh of a Santa Claus who already understands everything about the world of objects. What I like about this particular approach is that it doesn't consider matter to be inert and passive, but, instead, to be endowed with vital properties that render it active, productive, and creative without human intervention.

But I'm not one of those in the know, and this idea that matter can act by itself—that conscience and subjectivity may be nothing but accessories to the world—matches up with what I've always naïvely believed. It confirms to me that humans have no right or reason to keep themselves on their pedestal. Of course, the only things I know about this "new materialism" are what P.'s told me about it, but the fascination I feel is enough to make me believe my place in the universe is beside the wooden table, beside the tree, beside the stone that erupted from the ground during the frosty snap.

The dinner dishes are put away, the cat's in, I've brushed the calico, and P. is in his bedroom reading Graham Harman's *The Quadruple Object* or one of his other books about existential materiality that he'll tell me about tomorrow. It's bombyx time, the hour when the house sinks into shadow and I take refuge in my study to focus on an idea, a dream, an image that's important to me or that deserves attention as the day draws to a close. It's also the time of day that I'm alone with myself or the cat, who right now is washing himself in the armchair and taking particular care to clean away all traces of mud on his paws.

The La Languette notebook is sitting upside down on my desk, still open at page 3, the one on which I named Ferland and McMillan. This morning, after I reread the sentence about those two men, "The first will be called Ferland and the second McMillan," I tried to relegate it below the banality of the daily tasks—fixing the fence, painting the porch, pouring wine for dinner—but it never left me for a single second. It was right there in black and white, "McMillan, Ferland," "Ferland, McMillan," when P. was telling me about the book that had come in the mail for him, as the cat was chasing a chipmunk, when a branch fell off the maple tree, scraping the roof on the way down, when a deer crossed through the backyard and I thought of the nature-defying hunt Ferland and McMillan would have undertaken had I not abandoned the La Languette notebook on its third page.

And moreover, it seems that the story gestating in this notebook, after sketching out the basics near a frozen river criss-crossed with animal tracks, hadn't come to an end when I shut the notebook and put it away at the bottom of a drawer. Everything unfolded as if the tale, once it had been set in motion, had taken on a life of its own, though it might always have known a whimsical life of its own, regardless of whether or not I intervened, a life analogous to all these objects that have absolutely no need of me to exist and evolve. How else to explain why Heather is so afraid of Ferland and McMillan? The story continued without me — perhaps happened without me — and here I am back at the starting point again, needing to reconstruct the story if I am to learn what happened to Heather Thorne, Gilles Ferland, and Herb McMillan.

IV.

Torrential rain is beating down on Two Hill Lake, transforming the horizon into a foggy wall and obscuring the houses, the trees, even the lake. From my position halfway up the mountain, all I can see below me is a grey space, more or less oval in shape, with ragged edges, that the windshield wipers allow me to see intermittently. Parked at the opening of a barred road, I'm waiting for H. W. Thorne's rear lights to disappear into the rain before I go inspect his property again. When I see him take a right at the four-way stop, a perfect cross at the bottom of the slope and just like the four-way stop on the 4th Line, I interrupt the wipers' constant darting back and forth and turn the engine off.

Water is running down the windshield in sinuous waves, hiding the countryside and making the inside of the car feel like a watertight cube plunging to the bottom of a turbulent sea. Disturbed by the thought that the windows might give way, and an icy wave gush into the car, I grab my bag and rush out into the rain, where I breathe in the scent as joyously as someone who has just escaped asphyxiation. I pull my raincoat hood up over my hair, already soaked through, climb the last few metres up to

H. W. Thorne's property, and set off down the driveway leading to the house.

The rain is less intense under the tree cover, but the water that has accumulated on the branches is falling in heavy drops and crashes on my hood with a noise like gunshots. By the time I am in front of the house, the rain has intensified and I have to walk with my head bent over, one hand shielding my eyes, just to be able to see a little better. I take shelter under the awning on the east side of the house, where H. W. Thorne has stacked firewood, and look in my bag for a clean tissue to wipe off my glasses. When I put them back on again, I notice an enclave in the undergrowth, where several trees have been felled to install a bench made of granite blocks.

I head toward the enclave and catch sight of another block of granite in front of the bench, this one standing vertically—a tombstone with an inscription I can't clearly make out from this distance. I approach and walk around the bench to read the epitaph through my rain-spotted glasses. The words engraved on the stone read, "Heather Waverley Thorne, 1963–1980." Slightly stunned, I sit down on the bench and wait for the rain to stop.

V. has stuck a note to his door: "Out chopping wood. Back at four." From this I guess that he's waiting for someone and doesn't want to miss their visit. It's 3:45 by my watch, and apart from me there's not a living soul around. I decide to go sit on the patio. If someone else shows I'll give up my place and come back another time.

The low table has been cleared, and a fine layer of pollen covers its polished glass surface. With my index finger I write a few words on the table: "Heather Waverley Thorne, 1963–1980." Then I wipe my finger on my pants, where it leaves a yellowish trail, although a more lacklustre yellow than that of the daffodils growing in a circle at the bottom of the patio.

I'm quite surprised to see the flowers, because V., as far as I know, is not the gardening type. But do I even know V.? Discovering Heather's tombstone proves — contrary to what I'd concluded when I went through the village cemetery — that V. did not lie to me. It follows that he must either be a character I have created, or exist as a consequence of my desperately wanting to rely on the testimony of an old friend in order to understand what made up my past, just as I rely on P. to gauge the state of my mental health.

The noise of an engine makes me jump and I meet V. as I descend from the patio. A man I immediately recognize gets out of his truck. It's R. — V.'s brother — and he has come to tell me V. had an accident in the woods, nothing serious, but he won't be able to see me today. R. has just driven V. to the emergency room in the nearest town, and he'll probably have to hang around for a few hours before a doctor lets him leave.

I listen to R.'s explanations and don't interrupt, all the while staring at the V-shaped notch between his eyebrows and trying to remember if V. has the same mark. Then I look at his hands again, they're powerful and rough, and tell him he's got the wrong person, that I'm not the person V. was expecting.

R. corrects me and says that V.'s message was clearly intended for me. "You're Beverley, right? Beverley Simons?" I lower my head so he doesn't notice my face's sudden pallor and murmur to myself that perhaps I am called Beverley—of course—*Beverley Simons*.

I carry the bags of soil we bought at the hardware store over to the house, panting like an ox. P. tries to help, but I won't let him. I want to exhaust myself physically so that I don't think any more. Once the bags are piled up near the entrance to the basement beneath the porch, I grab a shovel and try to dig a hole behind the house, wide and deep enough to plant a tree of an as-yet-undetermined species. (I'll decide tomorrow, when I go back to the Saint-Vital greenhouses.) With every strike of the shovel, I hit different-sized rocks that I have to pull out of the ground, either using a pick or hauling them out with both hands. Once I'm finished, I throw the rocks into the wheelbarrow and steer them over to the rock pile, where I tip out the wheelbarrow, swearing as I go. Then I start over, dig another hole, this time at the edge of the wood, where I've wanted to plant an azalea for a very long time.

When, finally, I go back inside, I toss my clothes in the laundry basket and take a shower. A trickle of brown water runs over the tiles, whirls around the plughole and then disappears into the network of pipes that run along the basement ceiling. I imagine its journey to the ditch where the light gush of it must disturb the dirty surface of the greasy water accumulated there. Next, I examine my hands and forearms, now marked with new cuts and a few scrapes revealing the delicate subcutaneous pink. I lather them with soap, so that the burning stops me from thinking, and sit down on the floor of the shower.

Legs pulled up against my body, I notice a few bruises forming on my right leg and hip, where I must have banged myself on the shovel or the pick, or used my weight to propel the wheelbarrow forward. My whole body is covered in grazes, bumps, and wounds; all the stigmata of country life and the novel I'm determined to write even as I order myself not to think.

I stay in the shower for another ten minutes or so, letting all those litres of water swirl pointlessly down the plughole, when P. knocks on the door of the bathroom to ask if everything's okay.

No, everything is not okay. My name is Beverley Simons. My name is Andrée A. My name is Heather Thorne and I died thirty-five years ago.

A hot, damp wind perfumed my bedroom this morning, imbued with scents hard to define: the hint of storms close by, and of aged wood; the smell of hay, grass, and barely blooming flowers. It roused an intangible feeling of happiness in me, straight out of childhood days when joy was pure and uncontaminated by the burdens of daily life, when all it took was a warm wind blowing the cotton curtains in my blue bedroom for me to know, without a shadow of a doubt, that the euphoria of play, of racing under the trees, would only be multiplied by a humidity that gave the smells body and made me feel the summer was tangible. I would walk in the dense air as if in my element, and nothing made me happier than seeing the curtains of my blue bedroom lifted by a wind heavy with the weight of its mixed perfumes.

Childhood is the fount of all things, I told myself, everything starts in those dawns and nights when the body is learning and the skin is open to the heat, wanting, according to the colour of the moment, to establish the foundations of laughter or of sadness. The thick morning air I was breathing in, as I petted the cat lazing on my bed, would not make me feel quite so euphoric if it hadn't come from such a distant place, if the scents it carried had not been augmented by memories of soft leaves and moist skins prefiguring the apprenticeship of the senses.

P. has just finished reading the first 139 pages of my manuscript. He has just come downstairs to say, "You're crazy," with a smile from ear to ear. The air is heavy and I am happy.

Where was I in 1980, the year Heather Waverley Thorne died? If I can rely on the few scraps of her story I know, then Heather Waverley died in winter — or rather, just before winter, before the cold snaps that discourage us from walking on isolated roads. That puts us, at the very most, two or three weeks before Christmas.

At that point of the year 1980 I was wandering the streets of a cold city thrown into shadow by its dour facades; I was studying Aristotelian logic, Kantian dualism, Federico Fellini's cinema, occasionally warming my stiff hands in bars redolent of beer, smoke, and boredom. But how can it be that I have no clear memory of that year? Why did nobody ever tell me about a young girl found dead in the snow, near an isolated road that I also walk on any time I come back to the village?

But who, in fact, *did* tell me that Heather Waverley Thorne was indeed found in the red snow of La Languette on a December morning? If Heather Thorne dies in an unfinished novel, murdered by a couple of men who went crazy, does this have anything to do with Heather

Waverley Thorne's passing? Can I conflate the two deaths, or are they distinct, one fictional and bloody, and the other caused by an accident or some illness I know nothing about?

The second cat's ashes arrived in a cardboard box with his name — "Beauboule" — written on it. Inside the cardboard box, decorated with a delicate paper flower and a few fake stones supposed to look like diamonds, was a wooden one also decorated with flowers, these ones a soft yellow, and a golden plaque that also had his name, "Beauboule," engraved on it. In the wooden box was a small white satin bag containing his ashes, a few plastic hearts that reflected the light, and an envelope with a little sachet that also had the cat's name — "Beauboule" — slipped inside it. The sachet contained a piece of fur with the mixed orange, gold, and red markings that only occur in cats. When I saw this lock of clean, well-brushed fur, I envisioned the whole cat once again, the cat in his entirety, and then the mouth and nose that emitted his own special *wormf, frounch, wormf,* sounds. Tears fell from my face onto the paper flowers.

From now on, every time I want to see the second cat again, I'll open the box, open the envelope, open the sachet, and speak his name, *Beauboule* — Beauboule, my love — and lose myself in the depths of his yellow eyes.

In my La Languette notebook I wrote that the events leading up to the story would occur at the end of November or the beginning of December — in other words, at the time of year when you're not sure, thanks to the cold and the snow, whether you should be calling it fall or, even though fall isn't officially over, winter.

Because of the incoherence of this country, and because I hadn't considered the season fully before covering the countryside with snow and having two men and a young girl meet deep in the heart of it, here I am flummoxed by the ambivalence of the northern climate. Should I imagine winter or fall when I refer to this unfinished season? It's exactly this sort of detail that, if you would rather not have to constantly explain yourself, must be clarified before you begin a story that will leave traces in the snow.

I am sitting on V.'s patio, under the parasol his brother recently set up, having had enough of roasting in the sun whenever he sat out there. He's the man who opened the door when I arrived and announced, somewhat brusquely, that V. had gone to the hospital to get his bandages changed after his accident in the woods. "I don't know how long it'll be before he's back," he added, anxious for me to leave. Seeing that I wasn't moving, he sighed and said I could wait if I wanted, and then hesitated before offering me a coffee. I agreed, reluctantly, because R.'s suddenly standoffish manners were making me uncomfortable. He was talking to me as if I were an intruder, not a girl from the village and an old friend of his only brother.

Keen to thaw R. out a little, I suggested that we be a little more informal. "Sure," he replied as he opened the parasol, "we can try it if you like, but I don't see what it will change." And he was right: given the nature of the situation nothing would change. I immediately regretted my decision to wait for V., and accepting the coffee I'd now have to drink, if only to meet R.'s diffidence with courtesy. And besides, what was R. doing at V.'s house? Didn't he have a job, a house, a family?

As if he'd read my mind, R. told me he'd moved into V.'s "until further notice." Apparently V. wasn't doing too well. Unexpected events had been bothering the man recently and R. was worried about him.

After alluding, vaguely, to the events that had upset his brother — an old lover, an old dream going up in flames — R. stared straight ahead at the undergrowth and silence fell between us. Beneath the parasol's orange light, his features were accentuated, and I could make out the sense of purpose that also characterized V.'s face. This was one way the two brothers were alike. It wasn't so much the shape of their noses or chins or the plumpness of their lips, but their gazes, their smiles, the way they moved their bodies, that indicated their shared lineage and close bond.

I was just about finished with my coffee when the noise of an engine travelled to us from the road. V. was back at last. I stood up to go greet him, but a man was already approaching the patio. Gilles Ferland. He was wearing a Red Sox ball cap and his face was covered in mosquito bites. We looked each other up and down for a few seconds, and then I announced to R. that I was going. As I passed Ferland, I could feel the current of animosity running through his muscles and felt as though I was in the darkness of Saint-Vital's 4th Line on a December evening. A shiver ran from my feet to my head and I jumped into my car.

Night is falling and I'm sitting with P. on the porch loveseat. I can hear spring frogs croaking in the swamp that separates our property from our neighbour's; their call reaches me through a kind of gelatinous screen distorting the sound. Mixed in with it is the almost deafening *ribbit, ribbit* of the wood frogs who've made their home in the forested area on the other side of the stream, so loud I can hardly hear what P. is telling me. I stretch toward the little red table in front of the loveseat for the bottle of Wild Turkey and help myself to another glass. I never drink bourbon, but tonight I need a rather tougher stimulant than my habitual after-dinner coffee.

P. doesn't dare tell me I've had too much to drink, because he's realized that I'm in one of those states where I can't hear or listen to anything. During dinner he'd tried to figure out why I was so on edge, but I didn't want to talk to him about Ferland, or R., afraid that he'd challenge me or accuse me of being paranoid. I changed the subject and brought it back to what we'd been discussing before we were distracted by a phone call and dragged back to our everyday preoccupations: the fence that needed to be put back up, the wild roses that need pruning, the porch we have to paint. I wanted to talk about the moon which had just risen behind the mountain and would soon be making the dogs howl. I wanted to describe to P. the hypothesis

143

which argues that Theia, a planetoid the size of Mars, collided with Earth to cause the formation of the satellite ruling our tides and our lunatics' moods.

I sketched out Theia's shape with my hands, and, as the first dogs started to howl, I watched the sky in which heaps of pulverized matter were flying, flaming rocks of fire that would explode and then merge in explosions muffled by the distance. For a moment I forgot all about Ferland, Heather, H. W. Thorne, and the others, instead imagining the stories I would write about how the stars came into being, deep in the core of a universe of infinite darkness into which my weightless body would ultimately drift.

Now I've fallen back down on the ground again, my feet resting on a wooden crate that looks further away with every sip of bourbon, each taste at the same time lengthening my interminable legs. At the end of my feet, I see Heather keeping watch over the woods from inside her car as she asks herself why the trees are swaying so, and where the two men are hiding—the two men she dreams about, leading her to scream to the point that she is jolted out of her sleep and compelled to position herself near the broken window that protects her no more against the bad weather than it does the covetous hands heading toward her through the unending forest and about to enter this zone outside of time over which the storm will soon break.

"Storm," I say to P. as I put my glass down on the red table, "we have to watch the storm," and I go to bed, my long legs vaulting me up the stairs that fade into the darkness.

In the collapsing bed, I tell myself that maybe Heather is right and perhaps she and I are stuck, like Schrödinger's cat — like the second cat could have been — in a place where we are simultaneously dead and alive. If this is the case then someone must apprehend us, between night and daylight, and confirm that we exist, if a delivery man is not to turn up at the house one fine day to give P. a box decorated with delicate flowers and the name "Heather" written on it.

It's raining on the 4th Line. I forgot to bring my raincoat, and all I have for protection is P.'s father's cap, the one P. bought for him on a trip to Martha's Vineyard. P. always leaves this cap, which has the logo of the famous Martha's Vineyard Black Dog sewn on it, in the car in case it rains, as it is doing today. I'm slightly uncomfortable wearing the cap of a dead person who is not a blood relation, but don't want to retrace my footsteps to put the Black Dog where it belongs, on one of the back seat's head rests, from where it can watch the road.

I walk with my head bowed, because the cap is too big for me and slips down over my forehead with every step I take, so far that the visor obstructs my view. I grope my way forward, watching the water drip from the visor onto the soaked ground, and tell myself I'm an idiot for wearing this cap that doesn't belong to me. I don't know if Heather will be near the Buick, or if she'll even want me in the vicinity, but I'm taking the chance because I need to see her, to touch her injuries and compare them with my own, and to hear her hoarse voice like my own. Basically, I need to know if there's really a corpse under the tombstone near H. W. Thorne's house, or if the young girl meant to be

146

there somehow outlived the mourning of her loved ones.

After leaving a very narrow, snaking path between the trees, I finally see the branches that were broken when Heather's car crashed through. I hurry in the direction of the accident and pull up sharply a few metres away from the Buick. Heather's upper body is framed in the broken window that still has a scrap of purple leather clinging to it. And she's pointing a gun at me.

For an instant, time stops. I can't hear the rain falling anymore, I no longer feel my clothes sticking to my skin, the mud has no smell, and I don't see Heather cocking the gun. When a bird, blue, maybe black, takes off from the roof of the car, I think the sound is a shot and crumple to the ground.

A band of yellow bleeding into red appears at the edge of the night, a corona surrounding the darkness as if the sun were setting at the same moment everywhere and spreading the hues of an impossible twilight across the bottom of the sky. If I didn't know it was an illusion, I'd have thought the end of days had arrived, annihilating the Earth in bursts of blinding colour.

Did Heather really shoot at me, did the bullet really pierce my leather jacket, or did the fear of dying make me anticipate the shot — and the shock its impact would cause?

For several long minutes, I was deaf, as happens to anyone when their senses are exposed to a super-loud explosion, and hurled to the ground with a searing pain in their chests. Night fell and I was still there, curled up on the spongy ground and waiting for coyotes surely attracted by the scent of blood to come shred my flesh.

I no longer remember how I got home, but excepting the bruise marbling my right breast — which hit a root when I fell — my chest is in one piece. I can't remember any of it anymore, except for Heather's face, white as plaster, and the noise of the gun that deafened me.

V.

Even though summer has arrived, an autumnal atmosphere blankets the entire countryside today. A fine cold drizzle spatters the windows and the wind is blowing so hard you'd think it wants to tear all the new leaves from the maples, their weakest branches bending over sharply before snapping back to their original position, shaking their heads like shackled animals.

Sitting in front of the blank page, I remember Heather's unblinking face as she pointed the gun at me and try to put it out of mind, focusing instead on the image of H. W. Thorne's truck disappearing into the night. I interrogate myself once more about the origins of this man claiming to belong to the same story as me, wondering by which obscure path or secret corridor he came out of the shadows and into the forest, and I decide, for lack of any more plausible option, that he simply came from the night—that night is where he was born and where he appeared, at the heart of the darkness I myself created, and into which, whether I want to or not, I shall have to plunge.

Since H. W. Thorne was born of darkness, I waited for night to fall before proceeding to his house. The rain had stopped, but the wind was still howling, pushing clouds through the sky that hid the moon before carrying on their northward race.

Thorne's truck was parked in front of the house, just as I expected. The naked bulb hanging in the hall cast light over the yard through which I walked with the impression of encountering floodlights installed by an adherent of jungle law who'd not hesitate to shoot at my slightest wrong move.

For a moment, the pain that had been throbbing in my chest by Heather's car resurfaced, and instinctively I brought my hand to my right breast. Convinced this sudden movement would trigger a barrage of bullets, I quickly crouched down and rolled outside the perimeter of light, my body entirely folded into the fetal position you instinctively adopt when an attack feels imminent. But no noise came from either the house or the woods. By the time I'd stopped panicking, two feet — two real feet — shod in heavy boots stood in front of me. Then a flashlight shone out, blinding me as I tried to identify the man who, towering over me, seemed even more imposing silhouetted against the hall light. "Get up," said the voice of H. W. Thorne. Then he turned off the flashlight and headed for the house.

The door was open when I climbed the few steps up to it, and H. W. Thorne was waiting for me in the small living room to the right of the front door, with a bottle of cheap gin between his legs. "Drink," he ordered, holding out the bottle to me as soon as I was sitting in the armchair facing his own. As I brought the bottle to my lips, the overpowering smell of the drink made me bilious, the alcohol burning my throat and then the centre of my chest, right beneath the spot where Heather's bullet would have entered. As I pulled the bottle away, I felt a little cold liquid dribble down my chin and neck and wet my t-shirt collar. I wiped my mouth with the back of my arm, like cowboys in saloons or crooks in noir films do, and took a deep breath. H. W. Thorne and I were ready to talk.

When P. smelled the traces of the cheap gin on my skin and neck, he asked if I'd been at the village hotel or getting drunk with Heather. I replied, "The man with the gun is born of the night," and, adding that I didn't feel like laughing, went upstairs to change.

Now P. is asleep, the cat is snoring in his armchair, the calico cat's just gone down to the basement, and I can see my hands tremble as I think back on my conversation with H. W. Thorne in the little living room where a photograph of Heather in hunting clothes occupied pride of place on the low table. I pointed at the photo, whose polished frame contrasted with the dust covering the table, and asked Thorne if she was his daughter. He took a big slug of the cheap gin, lowered his head, and said, "Yes, that's my daughter, Heather Waverley."

I had just asked the question for form's sake, because unconsciously I knew, ever since Heather inhaled the smell coming off the man with the gun—a mixture of forest, childhood, and peaceful days, rather like the smell trailing in my own father's wake—that H. W. Thorne had to be the man with broad shoulders who held her hand when she was a child and took her to see the hares on the La Languette trail. I had simply inverted the roles. In the story I was writing, it was the daughter, Heather Waverley, who was dead. But in the unwritten story, the father, the man with broad shoulders, was the one who had died.

This is the kind of ghost you have no interest in reviving, but then you describe a smell or draw a rough portrait, the ghost comes back to life, and you find yourself grappling with a stranger who's taken the father's place, and one daughter who's replaced another and must be eliminated for the world to achieve equilibrium once more, for no equilibrium is possible when the resuscitated body is not the person lying in the tomb.

According to H. W. Thorne, Heather Waverley died on December 7, 1980, though her body was only found on the 12th—this, after a strange journey that would flummox the coroner and prevent him from determining the exact time or even date of death.

It was a Sunday, one H. W. Thorne would never forget. Heather had gone for a walk in La Languette, as she did almost every Sunday afternoon. She'd taken her father's Buick and had parked near the crossroads at the foot of the little bridge that spans the river. At 3 p.m., H. W. Thorne felt a sharp pain in his chest and dropped his book, a John Irving novel Heather had given him. The book fell to his feet, in front of the same armchair in which he was presently sitting with, between his legs, the bottle of cheap gin he would mechanically lift to his lips as he told me what he knew of Heather Waverley's death — which was not much, in fact, what with all leads obfuscated and so much mystery still surrounding her death, even now, thirty-five years later. He was, however, sure of one thing: Heather had died at 3 p.m., when *The World According to Garp* hit the floor.

It's pointless trying to find a message in the book Heather chose to give to her father. John Irving's *The World According to Garp* was simply the first relatively neutral title that came to my mind as I wrote the preceding lines, not wanting anyone to strive for a connection between the novel Thorne was reading and the way the story unfolds. It's just a prop. I wanted Thorne to drop a book, any book, and for the sound of it falling to ring out as loud as the drama whipping Thorne's life. A glass would have done the job just as well, maybe a cup, or a pipe, which would have left a stain on the living room carpet. The broken or knocked-over glasses will come later.

I anticipate the scene in which the clear or amber liquid draws an indeterminate pattern near H. W. Thorne's armchair, and open my own copy of *The World According to Garp*, the yellowing cover showing its age. As I read the words I wrote on the flyleaf, I realize I was given this book in 1980 for a Christmas present around two weeks after Heather Waverley Thorne died. I'd forgotten this detail, just like I've forgotten almost everything about December 1980. Now I'm the one who drops the book, its dust jacket lands near the cat's armchair and I pray that the sound of it falling is not tolling the bell of another death.

July 1. Canada Day. I return to the cemetery, because the first of July is also my father's birthday. On his tombstone, the rain makes a pattern of long trees whose skinny trunks stand in relief against the black of the granite and form a grey forest evoking the sanctity of a cathedral. "Hi Dad, hi trees, happy birthday," I say, and, after saluting the caterpillar crawling along the horizontal beam of the cross that decorates the stone — "Hi caterpillar" — I leave the cemetery with tears stinging my eyes.

It's been a rotten spring and a shitty summer, that's what everyone keeps saying in the face of the continuing cold weather and the rain that never stops falling over the land, on the flooded fields, on the untended gardens, exacerbating the mood of the gloomiest among us. I join in this chorus of complaining, hoping for some sign of warmth, some respite for the flowers, for the animals, for the people. And yet this summer has already had moments of such beauty for which it has been worth enduring a couple of errant days of fall, especially those few minutes during which I crouched with my cat under the big maple, waiting for the storm to arrive.

It was only six o'clock, but already an unexpectedly dark evening was supplanting the dusk. Behind the hedge of rose bushes, black clouds whirled across the sky toward the village, and we could hear the distant grumblings that heralded the storm's imminence. The air was heavy, almost compressed, the maple leaves were barely rustling above our heads, and whatever weak light managed to pierce through the clouds had that amber tint I associate with the world's hazy beginnings. Then a flash of lightning ripped through the clouds behind the rose bushes and the sky vibrated with a rumbling that you could believe had arisen from depths incessantly rumbling without our even being aware of it.

Sheltered under the maple, the cat and I were happy, and then the wind rose furiously, forcing the rose bushes to lean over, whipping up the dust on the road, and transporting twigs, dead leaves and other, living ones ripped from the trees. In no time at all, we were soaked to the bone, the cat seriously annoyed and me still happy.

I know, I know, it rains a lot in this novel, and there's more rain to come. I can't help it. All I have to do is open the manuscript, and the skies open too, spotting the pages with either tiny scattered dots or bigger patches summing up the climate of the writing hours in which I seek the respite of grey mornings.

H. W. Thorne was practically drunk when he agreed to talk to me about December 7, 1980. After dropping *The World According to Garp*, still open at page 132, he'd put on his coat and boots and hightailed it over to his nearest neighbour's, a young man named Vince Morissette who'd recently moved into a house about a kilometre away from his own. Seeing Thorne in such an anxious state, Morissette dressed quickly and accompanied him to La Languette, cursing the mounting storm. The two men peering through the windshield could barely see twenty feet in front of them; nevertheless, Thorne begged his young neighbour to drive faster, even as the mixture of hail and snow made the roads slippery, and threatened, with every gust of wind, to send them careening off the road.

The light was fading when they saw Thorne's Buick near the crossroads where Heather had parked. Before Morissette's car had even come to a halt, Thorne had opened his door and was running toward the Buick, hoping that Heather Waverley was sheltering there and waiting for the storm to ease off. The car was empty, but Heather's red tuque she refused to wear three-quarters of the time, preferring to expose her hair to the wind and freeze her ears, lay on the passenger seat. This was the tuque they would give the dogs to sniff when it became clear that Heather Waverley Thorne had disappeared.

Still confident they'd be able to find Heather before it was necessary to call in the dogs, Thorne and Morissette marched around La Languette calling "Heather" and "Heather Waverley" until it was dark and the wind, blowing through the trees with a sinister creaking, carried their cries away. At 6 p.m. Morissette, who was now as worried as Thorne, begged him to stay where he was and went to the village for reinforcements. One missing person was plenty.

At 4 a.m. Thorne was forcefully taken back to his house before he died of cold or gave himself a heart attack, but the search continued until the dogs arrived, the northeasterly wind still blowing through the trees with a sinister creaking.

I'm looking at one of the sections of the fence P. and I repaired last summer and that we'll need to strengthen some more, because nature moves, because the ground we rely on for stability is in constant motion, our own balance nothing but an illusion. On one of the posts partly hidden by the lower branches of our single solitary oak, stands an angel. I saw it the day before yesterday, and again yesterday—and it's still there, a white oblong shape that could well be the silhouette of a plaster Virgin Mary.

I bend down for a better view, unable to work out whether it's an angel or a Virgin. At first, I tell myself it's a Virgin angel, and then I correct myself because I've been told that angels don't have a sex. A Virgin turned angel, then, watching over the birds, the undergrowth, the oak, and who'll watch over Beauboule, the second cat, when we spread his ashes at the foot of it.

I point out the pure white shape perching on the fence to P. "It's a bit of stripped wood," he says, staring at the amber light coming through the glass of bourbon he's holding in front of him. "No," I say, "it's an angel, a Virgin covering herself with her wings."

Lying on the back seat of her Buick with the gun at her feet, Heather Thorne moves in her sleep. Through the blinding gusts of her nightmare, she can hear men calling her name, getting louder and closer, "Heather," "Heather Waverley." *Here*, she tries to answer, *I'm here*, but no sound escapes her mouth. On the verge of panicking, she realizes that the "here" she's talking about is somewhere in the sky beyond the gusts. A sharp feeling of nausea immediately takes hold of her, because only the souls of the dead fly higher than the wind like this, only spirits fading into the black sky, unable to do anything but scream the memory they still have of words.

I'm here, she murmurs, and then she falls, falls, falls, and wakes up, soaked in sweat, to the morning song of buntings and jays.

I've just filled up the bird feeders and am sitting for a moment on the stone steps that descend through the arch between rock gardens, where wildflowers and cultivated plants are intertwined, contesting the few metres bordered by the two piles of rocks and going beyond them to colonize the ground around: hostas, phlox, mugwort, buttercups, hawkweed, and so on. Fifteen or more varieties, some seeded or planted by me, others by our predecessors, others still by the wind and animals.

Sometimes I wish this was all I had to do — sow, plant, weed, sow again — for the simple pleasure of watching shoots burst through the ground, the buds appearing, then flowers emerging from them; not having to worry about Heather, or Vince Morissette, who has been on my mind ever since H. W. Thorne described to me how he set off with him to look for Heather on December 7, 1980.

I wonder why, when I was looking for the man with the gun, V. never mentioned H. W. Thorne; why he steered my attention toward the two men from the neighbouring village, one of whom might have been Heather's assailant — or his double, his carbon copy, what do I know? It was as if he wanted to set me off in a different direction, for me to discover for myself which pawns I'd placed on the chessboard, and how the game had been played without my knowledge.

The day had barely begun, but I'd go visit him as soon as the sun was high enough for him to offer me a beer and for the two of us to continue our conversation like two old friends: Bev, short for Beverley, and V., short for Vince or Vincent Morissette.

———

"Vincent's not well," his brother said to me as he opened the door. "He doesn't want any visitors." For a moment I was speechless. As I was getting out of my car I'd seen Vince on the patio out back, eating peanuts and tossing the shells to the ground. I ignored R., who seemed to be inventing a pretext to stop me from seeing Vince every time I visited. Instead, I walked around the house and sat down next to Vince. "We need to talk," I said with no preamble, and Vince signalled to his brother to leave us alone, even though R. was ready to grab me by the scruff of the neck and send me back to where I'd come from like some ne'er-do-well.

Reluctantly, R. went inside the house, though not before shooting me a killer look that I ignored. Vince picked up the pitcher of sangria sitting among the peanut shells by his feet and poured me a glass. After he clinked his glass against mine, pointing at the bowl of peanuts and telling me to help myself, he asked, politely, since he already knew perfectly well, what it was I wanted to discuss. When I mentioned Heather's name, he murmured, "Why wake the dead, Bev?" unaware that sometimes the dead wake themselves up and that we have no choice but to reintegrate them into the world of the living. So I paid no heed to his objection and brought up the subject of the storm, the northeasterly wind and its sinister whistlings, so that Vince would understand I didn't intend to give up.

We talked over one glass of sangria after another until R. came to ask Vince if he was hungry. There were a couple of steaks in the fridge waiting for someone to do them justice, he said, and R. was so hungry he could eat a horse. "Just wait a few more minutes," Vince said, and offered to share a steak with me. I said thank you and then reminded him I didn't eat any meat—no flesh other than my characters', but he didn't get it because he still thought I was Bev. I didn't think it was a good idea to disabuse him of the notion, as I barely knew myself quite who I was anymore.

I told Vince to eat and rest, because I'd noticed that he seemed to be suffering as we talked, though he was trying to hide it and brushed away any questions of mine about the state of his health. "Take care, amigo," I added, before leaving without saying goodbye to R., who was watching me from the window over the sink as if he wanted to cast a spell on me, turn me to stone just by looking.

I gave him the finger so we were equal, and then drove off at full throttle, only to slow down after the first turn once I was out of his sight. Then I forced myself not to go faster than fifty, because those few glasses of sangria I'd knocked back were blurring the road my shining eyes were struggling to follow, the colours of the countryside too luminous to be real. At the intersection with Route 263, I accelerated slightly. I took the Cordon bend as though it were a long skating rink, at the end of which I'd end up at my house trying to process, in the quiet of my study, the information—disturbing to say the least—that Vince had provided.

———

When I got back, P. was watching an old *Star Trek* episode, and I took advantage of his eyes being glued to the television screen to avoid him. "I need to pee, it's urgent," I pretended, rushing into the bathroom. In actual fact I wanted to examine myself in a mirror bigger than the one in the car to see if my bloodshot eyes were less disconcerting from further away. This was not the case. I splashed my face with cold water, put a few drops of Visine into my eyes, and swallowed a quarter-bottle of mouthwash. I didn't want P. to conclude that every time I came back from seeing Vince or H. W. Thorne or any of my characters, as he thought of them, my breath stank of alcohol. I might as well not have bothered: the alcohol in the mouthwash amplified the alcohol in the sangria, and made it seem as though I'd been drinking aftershave.

I composed my face and left the bathroom to head to the fridge. "I'm going to peel some potatoes," I called out to P. "I had a couple glasses of sangria with Vince and I'm starving," but then on the counter I saw the ingredients P. had prepared for dinner, all lined up in a series of bowls arranged in order of height: garlic, not yet crushed, in the smallest; the next one for the olives; the third one for cheese, and so on. We were going to eat pasta that night and I was the one who'd asked for it, which I'd forgotten in the rush to conceal my drunkenness.

"Is something wrong?" P. asked, as I was putting the potatoes back in the fridge. "Everything's great," I lied. "I'm hungry. When are we eating?" I said, like a teenager who thinks food makes itself and wants nothing else — wants to eat, not talk, and especially not to talk about the guy who's just informed her that fictional characters aren't brought by the stork.

Eventually I fed the cats, set the table, and helped P. make the pasta. I even chose the music to listen to during dinner — the soundtrack to *Apocalypse Now*. I wanted to hear "The End" by The Doors, playing through the helicopter noises and the soldiers whistling to the tune of "Suzie Q." As the brass was starting up "The Ride of the Valkyries," I announced to P. that from now on V. would be called Vince, short for Vincent, because H. W. Thorne had revealed his name and I was fed up with the accumulation of so many initials perforating my sentences with a whole bunch of little dots. If I was in possession of three or four names, it was only fair that V. should be allowed at least one.

P. coyly avoided asking me when, finally, I would call him Pierre. Instead, he talked about the Philip K. Dick novel he'd started reading the day before yesterday, a story about a planet that people thought initially was some kind of work camp or penal colony, but which didn't actually exist. "In fact," P. continued, taking a sip of his wine, "the people supposedly sent to this planet were propelled into another temporal dimension, one of the twelve Dick imagined and—"

And that's where I lost him. I was thinking about what Vince had told me that afternoon, about the drama I'd perhaps put in play thirty-five years after it occurred, and I thought to myself that Dick and I probably had a few things in common, the difference being that he could legitimately call himself a science-fiction or futurist writer, while I was swimming in cold, hard reality.

The hour of the bombyx was dragging on and I was starting to worry about the cat, who hadn't come when I called out to him from the darkened porch, where I'd heard two of the little Alberts or Albertes munching up the scraps that had fallen from the bird feeder. I'd become obsessed. I was picturing the cat confronting a lynx, as he has done before, or trying to run from a pack of coyotes. Anxiously, I was looking forward to the moment when I could sit at my desk and think over the implications of Vince's revelations, but the images of the cat I was entertaining, a combination of horror movie and wildlife documentary, were preventing me from thinking clearly about what he had told me.

According to Vince, the storm had lasted for nearly four days, every passing hour reducing the chances of finding Heather Waverley alive. The police had joined the search, dogs had sniffed the red tuque and the other clothes that H. W. Thorne, whom nobody had been able to keep at home, was carrying in a large white plastic bag decorated with yellow flowers strangely contrasting with the wintry scenery. Snowmobilers who'd heard about the crisis arrived from surrounding villages and even further away, in such numbers that La Languette became a screaming forest in which the rumbling of the machines mingled with the whistling of the wind, but nobody had found any trace of Heather.

It was only on December 12, two days after the storm ended, that the body was found, leaning against a tree on the edge of a clearing through which so many snowmobilers had travelled that not a single square metre of its ground had been spared the chewing of their vehicles' caterpillar tracks.

At the time, it was concluded that Heather had not died on December 7, as her father claimed, but had wandered for another five days, battling hunger, cold, and the violent winds, finally dying just a few hours before she was found, which only made her death more shocking and the notion of H. W. Thorne's suffering more intense. Further examination of the body and clothes would reveal, however, that Heather Waverley's journey to the clearing had been much more complicated.

The lynx that had confronted the cat was actually a young female called Sylvette who used to wander around our house two years ago, likely on the hunt for a male with whom she could mate and deciding that the cat would do. The wildlife agents didn't believe what we told them, because as a rule lynx don't approach houses, and as a rule cats don't attack lynx, but we have the photos, so there.

I'm sitting cross-legged under a spruce tree whittling a stick with a penknife P. gave me, a Smith & Wesson Special Tactical, its black blade featuring several serrations whose purpose I don't understand. P. claims that people who live surrounded by forest should always have a penknife to defend themselves and ensure their survival, but also for the thousand little tasks that require a sharp blade.

The risks of getting lost in the forest before I hit the 1st or the 6th Line were basically nil, and the chances of my attacking a bear with a three-inch blade non-existent; I use the knife to cut branches, clean my nails, open bottles, or simply pass the time, as I'm doing this morning, sitting under a spruce and sculpting an angel head that resembles, or at least I hope it does, the Virgin angel perched behind the oak. The angel's head, like my own face, is paler by the day even though I'm exposing myself to the July sun every time I work in the garden, cut the grass, put up a fence panel, or simply sip a cup of tea on the porch behind the house, daylight bearing down on it from the middle of the morning until 5 or 6 pm.

I'm dematerializing, you might say, for the benefit of Heather and H. W. Thorne, whose initials, for all I know, could denote a Henry Walter, Hank William, Harold Wayne, or even Henry William, Hank Walter, and so on. Among all the possible combinations, none seem right. So I decide, until further notice, to call him Howard— Howard Wayne Thorne—Howard W. for short.

I raise my eyes to the tops of the pines and cry, "My name is Howard, Howard Wayne!" At the same instant, the knife in my grip slips on the piece of wood and wrecks the head of the angel I'm clumsily trying to make. A few drops of blood pearl at the tip of my index finger and are quickly absorbed by the angel's damaged head as it turns slowly into a red Virgin. I let the blood flow and nail the piece of wood next to the white Virgin, who, with eyes closed and lips sealed, calmly looks over the ashes of a cat named Beauboule.

As I examined my pale face in the mirror, an old dream came back to me. I rifled through my notebooks to find the few words I'd written about the disturbing dream, and could only find this: "When the lakes start to dry up, memory is covered with rocks, and abandoned quays drift on the sand, then time itself is drying up, along with the thirsty bones."

According to the coroner's report, Heather Waverley Thorne had in fact been dead for some time when her body was discovered in the clearing, which meant that someone had carried her there to sit her up against a tree facing the rising sun. Examination of the body also revealed that Heather was no longer a virgin and had been subjected to attacks that led to fears that she had been raped. Yet strangely, neither her skin nor her clothes had any traces of blood or sperm. By all evidence, her attacker had scrupulously washed her body, underwear, and pants, suggesting that her assailant might have shut the corpse up in a cabin before bringing it back out into the cold.

The extremes of temperature, and the moving of Heather Waverley Thorne's body that had covered the tracks, explained why the coroner was unable to provide definitive information to the young girl's father, who swore he'd find the shit who'd murdered his child. Nobody doubted what he would do to the man, but nobody dared to try to make him see reason. Howard W. Thorne was ready to kill, and you can't stop an armed man set on revenge unless you want to become his first victim.

Vince and the coroner talked about the assailant. Howard W. Thorne swore the man responsible for Heather Waverley Thorne's death would pay for his crime. Vince, the coroner, and Thorne believed a single individual had attacked Heather. Heather wrote, "The first is called Ferland and the second McMillan." Only Heather and I know the truth of it.

Once again, I'm sitting with Howard W. Thorne, and now I understand the mixture of rage and sadness that hardens his features. A bottle of scotch he was swigging from directly had replaced the forty-ouncer of cheap gin. He held the bottle out to me, but I refused it with a wave, even though I was extremely thirsty. I wanted to keep my ideas straight and, specifically, not to blurt out Ferland and McMillan's names in a moment of drunkenness for fear of setting off a bloodbath that would stain me as well, and make me a pariah in the whole county. If Howard W. Thorne, along with Vince and everyone else who'd witnessed the events in 1980, believed that Heather was the victim of a single attacker, then I needed to leave him with his erroneous belief until I was able to shed light on Ferland and McMillan's part in her death — and until I understood exactly how the pair had managed to evade the police investigation and Thorne's dogged searches.

"Could be that bastard's dead too," murmurs Howard W. Thorne, after a diatribe about the murderer's cowardice.

I can feel, in his voice, the bitterness that has grown over the years and made his breath taste of the bile he tries to eliminate by gargling alcohol. "A shit like that doesn't deserve a gentle death," he continues, the greatest joy Howard W. Thorne can imagine being to wrap his hands around the son-of-a-bitch's throat until he begs for mercy and confesses to the crime. Afterwards, he'd take all the time necessary to make him regret ever having set eyes on Thorne's daughter.

Howard W. Thorne's expression is glassy and remote, so consumed is he by the desire for revenge. He goes on to say there is no torture he's not imagined in all these years of pursuing a shadow, that there isn't a face in the region whose features he hasn't scrutinized until his quarry blushed, sometimes to the point of Thorne losing it in trying to discern some trace of shame or remorse, a flicker of the assailant's eyes, that would betray his fear — or, worse, the bravado of someone who feels invulnerable. "But the sonofabitch disguised his tricks so well he's been able to live in full view of the world," Thorne spits out, thumping a fist on the arm of his chair. "As if he'd done nothing wrong, still fucking his wife, still laughing with his pals around a table of full glasses and empty bottles, still driving his kids to school and licking the priest's ass every Easter.

"*Tabarnak*," he shouts, and then throws his glass against the wall, just missing me. He mumbles an apology, puts his head in his hands, and then staggers over to pick up the pieces of broken glass, which aren't the first pieces he's had to pick up, because I can see, on the wall where the glass smashed, brownish stains commemorating Howard W. Thorne's numerous impotent rages.

I'm wondering if I should help, or whether my interference would simply fan the flames of his fury, when I spot a different photograph lying flat on Thorne's coffee table. Within its white frame are a dog, and a little girl wearing a blue dress: Jackson and Heather one summer's day. It makes my blood run cold, because I recognize the photograph in which I appear on a hot summer's day with my dog Jeff, a photograph I had thought was lost.

I'm leaning over the photo when Thorne returns with a rag, broom, and dustpan. I point at the photo with a trembling finger, hoping he'll enlighten me about its origins, but just at that moment someone knocks at the door — three little taps followed by a big thump, like some kind of code. Howard W. Thorne looks at his watch and then puts down the broom, rag, and dustpan, takes me by the arm and ushers me out the back door, obviously not keen for me to meet his visitor. I try to protest, but the door closes on me with a dry slam, and I stand there, in the dark, listening to my heart beating.

Lasiurus borealis, commonly known as the Eastern red bat, likes hanging from trees, where it can be mistaken for dead leaves. I can see three or four of them around me, swinging from the end of a branch and then letting go to drop toward the ground or launch themselves on their erratic flight into the night, catching, as they go, a specimen of

Lymantria dispar, *Olceclostera angelica*, or any of the other moths whose names I don't know.

The hour of the bombyx has arrived, but no lamp lights the undergrowth through which I am making my way in the hope of finding a lookout spot from which to survey Howard W. Thorne's visitor. A wasted effort. The curtains are drawn, and all I can make out are two silhouettes moving from one window to the next as they proceed from the front to the back of the house. Then the patio light flickers on, and Thorne comes out and sits down, followed by Vince, who's carrying a bottle and two glasses.

Surrounded by bombyx hurling themselves at the light bulb above their heads, the two men talk in low voices, and from where I am lying in wait, all I can hear are low murmurs and the occasional burst of laughter. I examine the surroundings and decide that if I want to hear their conversation I need to move out into the open. Instead, I decide to go home and wait to be a part of the parallel story that Vince and Howard W. Thorne are writing. As I skirt around the house, I hear a name, *Howard*, rising above the squeaking of the *Lasiurus borealis*.

Back home, I write in my notebook: "Howard," "Howard Wayne Thorne," to establish once and for all H. W. Thorne's identity. Then I sit down in the black leather armchair near the cat's chair, from where I can watch the undergrowth at night. Through the motionless branches, fragments of the dream, a brief summary of which I'd recorded in one of the notebooks, comes to mind with startling precision, given that the dream happened several months ago. I'd been at Lake Saint-François, where I spent my childhood summers. The sky was overcast, though perhaps it was simply that the atmosphere was dusty, the clarity of the day diminished by the fine powder rising from the arid banks. I was walking close to where the lake had been; all I could see in front of me were a depression in the sand and rocks that disappeared into the horizon. My childhood was done. I was becoming old and dried out, just like the lake's furrowed depths.

But instead of giving in to this unavoidable reality, I grabbed hold of the docks meandering out over the sand in the hope they might lead to some river where I could soak my bones and renew my youthful suppleness. In vain. I woke up on a bed of rocks over which no river would ever flow again.

It was, I think, on this day that I went to La Languette and imagined, near the riverbed where just a thin trickle of water snaked between the stony banks, the tragic story of a young girl whose blood would entice me with the illusion that my hands were not yet so parched that I was no longer able to write.

It rained on my arid dream for a part of the night, and, this morning, the countryside lies beneath one of those stagnant fogs that remind me of the mists at Boundary Pond and their odour of fish and guts. I'm eight years old, I'm throwing stones into the lake, my father is standing on top of a ridge and observing the mountain like a man humbled by the majesty of the rock, and my name is Andrée.

―――――

"It's like remembering something from your childhood, and you're not sure if it's your memory, or a friend's memory, and then you realize sadly it's just some photo in an old book."

I am thinking about these words spoken by Dr. Abel Gideon, a character from the series *Hannibal* who no longer knows who he is, and who is questioning his own identity as he racks up murders in the hope of remembering.

It's like remembering something from your childhood . . . The photo on Howard W. Thorne's coffee table floats up above the misty landscape and I see myself again, scraped knees, running with Jeff, my beloved dog, at the edge of a field. At the end of this race, the camera click is heard, and child and dog together enter a book of pictures.

But the photo of the child and the dog might not belong to me. I concede the possibility that I've drawn the image from someone else's memory and appropriated it for myself—from my mother's memory, perhaps, as she posed with her dog Puppy, in a field of yellowed grass undulating to the same rhythm as the long black hair of this young woman in love. The thing that unsettles me is not my memory's ability to pillage other people's pasts, but the fact that I, like Abel Gideon, am racking up murders in order to find out who I am.

Nothing about reality seems real anymore. The middle of July is cold and the summer a lie. I've written that already, and catch myself believing it when the sun is shining and it's making sweat trickle down P.'s forehead. But the fall will be real, and already it is encroaching on the daisies' whiteness.

There are too many questions jostling for position in my head. I close my eyes and clasp my hands in front of my mouth, thumbs under my chin, in the posture people sometimes adopt for praying, and try to empty my mind so I can think, instead, about Heather's amnesia, wondering if her forgetting isn't characteristic of all fictional beings and if it's actually up to me to fill in the holes that perforate her memory.

But can memory really exist in someone who's just been born? What past do they actually have, these characters, already in their thirties, making their entrance on page 1 of a novel and being nudged toward the future along a trajectory that demands no backsliding? Is it possible to explain these characters on the basis of a hypothetical past, or is their existence only affected from the moment they arrive on the page, pressing the trigger of a gun, or throwing themselves into a river, the depth of which is the only thing that will determine the narrative?

My answer is simple: a character only exists from the moment they slip into a sentence, and I don't yet know if Heather Waverley Thorne fits this schema—if she started existing when her Buick appeared at the top of the slope on the 4th Line, or if her past eludes fiction, and because of this eludes me too. If this is the case, then Heather's amnesia is real, and my ignorance the result of her amnesia.

I've just had my first coffee of the morning on the porch and I'm breathing in the smell of my sun-warmed skin, resolving to take a long-overdue vacation during which this is all I shall do—warm my skin, breathe in the scent of P.'s, read under the trees, walk in the summer exuberance—nothing but slow activities permitting my tired body to rest a little. I'd have difficulty leaving Heather in limbo for a few days, but she'd follow me in my dreaming next to the fields, and benefit from a rest that would also benefit the novel; I've noticed that the text is showing signs of my fatigue and is likely to soon be mired in the same heaviness into which my body is sinking if I don't act.

I've taken this decision because of the lightness of the air, and the exquisite flavour of the coffee P. had made for me, though also because of the writer Hélène M., who always stood up against injustice but who died a couple of weeks ago because she smoked too much, lived too much, and very probably didn't give her frail body enough repose.

When P. read about her death in the paper and told me, I behaved just as I did this morning. I left the breakfast table, that time with my lips trembling slightly, bereft of the right words to describe the whiteness suddenly surrounding me, and I went to drink my coffee outside. As I lit a cigarette in Hélène's memory, I told myself my turn would come, that in time my own horizon would be lost in a grim sky the exact shade of cancer: anthracite grey or pitch black.

Before it's too late for the wind to blow away the clouds already closing in on me, I'm going to award myself a few carefree days, calm hours for my left hand to relax and for me to think of Hélène, telling myself that surely someone, somewhere, would write for her, "Lone-Angel / I will perform a ceremony for you," just as she had written for her sister Thérèse, who died before Hélène did under the falling ash of such an anthracite sky.

And as for my vacation, it will begin with your fleeting image, Hélène, with the angel I will draw for you on the wooden fence, and afterwards that of a happy child and dog on glorious July day.

VI.

O f those few days during which I put down my manuscript over the photograph of a child running with her dog, I will retain the memory of the waters of the Samson River, near the U.S. border, snaking around enormous rocks I wanted to climb, stretching my full length over them, with my back against the warmth of the rock. I will take, from those few days, the huge disappointment of not having climbed them, of not having planted my bare feet on the hot stone, of having behaved as if I were old even though my legs still tingle with a desire to jump, clasp the wind, and roll down to the foot of hills where eternity opens.

But I'll go back. Next year, I'll go back. I'll find the road I took to the river once more, I'll park near the bridge, I'll take off my sandals or running shoes, and I'll climb. When I will still be young.

The rushing noise of the Samson River was still enveloping me when I sat down at my desk to find Heather again. It was 8:25 in the evening and to one side of the road there was a rainbow, facing the sunset and the dark mass of cloud heading toward the last patches of blue sky. Despite the approaching storm, a few white-throated sparrows carried on singing, and the cat remained lying in wait beneath the cedars. As for the calico, she'd taken shelter in the basement, and the second cat, Beauboule, was materializing in the clouds. I was following the trace of his ginger tail when, announcing the deluge, the first drops of rain hit the windows and a flash of lightning tore through what remained of the blue to the north

I put my pen down on the page, where a few *Lasiurus borealis* lie scattered among the bombyx, and hurried outside. Streaks of yellow and pink were reflected in the wet asphalt, reflections before the storm, and suddenly I could no longer hear the sparrows. The din was here, sovereign in the windswept branches.

"None of this is real," I told myself as the cat ran under the porch. I turned around. The house was red and black.

Another vacation memory: where the sunset meets the north, clouds, like a broad expanse of sand lapped at by a lazy sea, roll out in their wrinkled state before night falls.

I explain to P. that perhaps the only way to know what really happened to Heather involves putting myself in her place and reliving her death. "But," he says, "isn't that what you do with all the characters whose death you decree?" I set him straight and remind him that Heather was already dead when I met her, that I hadn't planned her death, since it resulted from events which occurred before the story—back when the idea of our possible end was not a part of the future we anticipated.

"If I relive Heather's death then I'll remember," I concluded, clearing the table and not worried about the danger this identity theft might bring, not considering that effectively I might die in place of Heather, whom I would consequently abandon to a limbo in which she would be neither dead nor alive.

Native plants have invaded the part of the hill where, last year, I planted seeds of flowers that could not possibly compete with the robustness of the indigenous ones. So, pointlessly, I watch for the flowering of poppies and those delicate little mauve flowers whose name I can't recall and whose appearance I will consequently forget, for lack of being able to locate a picture of them after consulting the index of some book about wildflowers.

Still, every morning I lean out of the window looking out over the hill in the hope of noticing a few spots of red or mauve bursting through the green. I'll do this until the end of the summer—lean out of the window, push aside the tall weeds as I walk the circumference of the little hill—because hope is such that it denies the irrevocable: he will come, he will come, one morning I will see his outline at the end of the field, we tell ourselves, when the lover waited for in this way never comes.

Vince was fixing his fence when I parked outside his house. His face was wet, his t-shirt stained with sweat, and I'd never seen him so pale. I put his state down to the sleepless night he'd spent drinking and talking with Howard W. Thorne, on page 174 of the manuscript, and offered him the bottle of water I take everywhere in my bag. "You could do with getting some sun," he gasped after he'd swallowed half the bottle, "you're getting paler by the second." And right then I must have turned even paler—was my colour draining into Vince, or, conversely, was he communicating his pallor to me? I was just trying to work out the moment at which I'd started losing my colour when he interrupted my thoughts and led me into the house, where we could talk more comfortably.

He sat me down in the living room, went off for a minute to change into some dry clothes, and then, his hand shaking, gave me a coffee and asked how I was doing. I said, "Same as you, I suppose," showing him my own trembling hand. Then I told him about the photo I'd seen in Thorne's living room, and about how the dog in it looked like Jeff, the dog I had when I was a child. "Jackson," mumbled Vince, who then fell into silence, as if my mentioning the dog had sent him back to a time for which he was nostalgic, a time of untroubled days, though they may not have seemed that way at the time, but which we yearn for when we are capable of measuring the degrees of our insouciance. Then he got up to go look in the bottom drawer of a wooden chest, from which he pulled out a photo that he placed in front of me.

The photograph, covered in thin plastic like everything we want to keep free of dust, dirt, and damp, was of

Heather, Vince, and Jackson standing by the La Languette wayside cross just as fall was turning to winter. Heather, barely any shorter than Vince, was resting her head on his shoulder, and they were both smiling at Jackson, who, standing in front of them, seemed to be begging for their attention. The photo had been taken three days before Jackson died — run over by a truck on the mountain roads — and eleven days before Heather did.

've just driven five hundred kilometres under a merciless sun and I'm sitting on a quay near a river that hereabouts is known as a sea, listening to the rising tide. It hasn't been dark for long, and a few walkers are strolling hand in hand along the quay. I put my notebook down on the concrete platform and realize I'm the only person not holding someone's hand. It doesn't make me sad. If P. was here, I wouldn't be holding his hand anyway, because I hate hands that stop you moving your arms freely and take their grip in a manner suggesting possession. P. knows it, just as he knows I can only be his if he doesn't put a ring on my finger or the weight of his arm on my shoulder. That's how it will be until the end. I want to collapse alone and with my hands free, near a man — P. — who'll let me sink into the slow-moving earth.

I interrupt my work for a few moments and go to the patio doors that look onto the backyard, go back to my desk, back to the door, and then take a jar of pistachios out of the pantry and snack on them frantically, licking the salt off my fingers as I go and watching the starlings search for insects in the shorn grass. I haven't written for two or three weeks, it feels like five, and the reality of this is causing me anguish. I need to move, to ease the tension, eat, chase away the flies bothering me, the prickling in my legs, before I am able to return to that river, that sea, the couples walking in the dark.

On the shingle beach, I couldn't take my eyes off the white splash of a bird that stood out against the black sand. Everything pointed toward the bird's dying — its isolation, its immobility, its diminishing whiteness — and I tried, while not taking my eyes off it, to make it understand that it wasn't alone, that when the sea washed over it there'd be a witness to its last flight, and then a couple walked by, hands intertwined, and I abandoned the bird, which was perhaps just one of those free spirits defying the laws of its species and therefore destined to solitude. I gave it one last look and headed toward the far end of the quay.

I'd been in the seaside village because, the following day, I was due to give a reading from my latest novel, but the power of the river had taken me away from *Boundary* just as it took me away from Heather, Vince, and Howard W. Thorne. The only character the sea didn't submerge was P., whom I would tell about the bird as he described, in turn, the network of rivers that waters our country- side; whom I would tell about the smell of iodine, and the feeling of well-being, of the isolation that the increas- ingly deserted quay inspired in me — just me at one end, a shadow that, had you not read such peace in her posture, you might have believed was about to wade into the foam.

Leaning on the piled-up stones protecting the quay from the sea's repeated assaults, I watched the waves cresting, white in the immense darkness, telling myself that their parallel lines were perhaps only the result of our capacity and desire to make order of chaos.

Strangely, I felt at home, in my element, perhaps because of the waves' regularity, which apparently echoes the rhythm of our breathing. I filled my lungs with salty air, endeavouring to conform to the cadence of the sea, the roaring of which seemed to emanate from further away than the waves—as if they'd actually broken before hitting the rocks and the blast preceded the collision that would ultimately split and disperse a force that only had cohesion in its plurality.

Fascinated by the roaring, the sounds of wet shells, and the rumbles of thunder ripping through the darkness, I closed my eyes and understood that I was hearing the echo of a primordial breaching.

The next day, in an enormous garden, I shouted, "Who's there? Who's fucking there?" channelling Zaza Mulligan, the first girl to die in *Boundary*. Afterward, I hit the road again under another baking sun. Hundreds of kilometres from the sea, Heather was waiting for me with her head on Vince's shoulder at the intersection of the 1st Line and La Languette, in front of a wayside cross reminding us that others had believed in resurrection before us.

Once I was back in the village I found Vince, who'd not moved since I left and was gazing sadly at the photo propped up in front of him. It hardly needed a genius to work out that Vince, despite being a few years older than Heather, was madly in love with her, and that she felt the same way about him.

I understood now why Vince preferred not to rehash the circumstances of Heather's death. The pain was still there, and it would never go away, because the story of Vince and Heather was one of those unfinished ones that you never stop wondering about, wondering what might have happened had the other person survived, had the story continued, had there been children in the story, two or three little blond or brown heads that could have given it a different meaning. And I understood why Vince never told Howard Thorne about the relationship he had with his daughter. He was afraid of stoking Thorne's anger, of being cursed as a fucking bastard and an abuser of young girls before having his jaw broken and being thrown out of the house like so much trash. Their friendship had been born of a drama and a lie that forbade Vince from sharing in Thorne's grief and joining his anger to Thorne's.

"I would never have hurt her," Vince muttered, and then, once again, he referred to the moment when, on December 7, 1980, Thorne knocked at his door and the two of them set off to search for Heather, Vince as worried as Thorne was, but forced to hide it and pretend Heather was no more than Thorne's daughter to him, and that he was accompanying him to stop the man from going crazy.

"I nearly went crazy myself," said Vince, and then he stared at the photo again, in which none of the imminent drama was prefigured, just like all those pictures of smiling people with no idea that, the very next day, they'll die in a car accident or from a heart attack. Like in that picture of my father looking so content in the moment before he died—a photo that doesn't exist, that nobody ever took, but which is nevertheless one of the most vivid in the album I've accumulated over the years: Dad, fifty years old, leaping up from the postage-stamp-sized lawn in front of our house onto the porch whose cement has only just dried, laughing in the unrestrained way of men who have their whole future in front of them.

I stretched out my hand to pick up the photo of Heather, Vince, and Jackson, suddenly wondering who'd taken the snap. I asked Vince, who said it was his brother, R., who'd sought to immortalize the moment. I held back the swear word rising to my lips and examined the luminosity of the photo, gauged the angle from which it had been taken, the distance between photographer and subject, and then let it fly: "*Calvaire!*"

There was no doubt in my mind: the photo was the

work of a young man in love, of a teenager secretly lusting after his brother's girlfriend.

The following day was very strange. From the minute I woke up, I had the curious sensation that my vision was warping textures, corners, and colours, that I could see the people around me with X-ray vision and anticipate their movements. I was watching the cat and realized I could make out the skeleton beneath its fur. I intuited the shadow stretching out across the kitchen floor before P. traversed the ray of sun beaming in through the patio doors; I could see the object hiding on the wooden table: a bowl, maybe a mask or a boomerang, ready to strike me in the face when I was least expecting it — this being the purpose for which the wood was destined.

I knew all this was an illusion, the result of my own hypersensitivity, but still I was unable to focus on my work or even to hold my pen, which was bending under the pressure of my fingers as if the material wanted to revert to its original form. So I decided to leave my desk and go weed the garden where, I hoped, I'd be able to wrestle with the questions vexing me since the previous day — with the possible implication of R. in Heather's disappearance, with R.'s curious attentiveness to Vince ever since Heather's shadow had reappeared in my wake, with the almost visceral hatred R. had evinced toward me after I'd interrupted his brother's otherwise placid existence.

I raked over the thousand and one questions on my mind until the mist turned to rain. Then I went back to my desk, cursing the day I'd let R., someone I barely knew, into Vince's house.

On my desk, the lamp had turned into a steel bird.

On this Sunday in late August, La Languette was deserted. No trucks, no cars, no ATVS. I parked, as I usually did, set back at a distance from the wayside cross—if I'm still able to say "as usual," because I'd not been back to La Languette since I'd met Heather. I should have returned as soon as the first scenes of the novel I'd outlined by the river came back to me, but I'd preferred to focus on Howard W. Thorne and on Vince, indirect witnesses to the drama, instead of going into the field and examining the ground for clues, proof, or other traces of the drama in question.

I realized how absurd all this was when I woke up that day and saw a hare scampering into the morning haze behind the house, the small animal's flight making me think of the dozens of hares we used to see leaping and bounding through La Languette when I was a girl and we'd go out in the mist to watch the animals leaving the woods. Taking the scurrying hare as a sign, I fed the cats, made myself a coffee, and, without even bothering to shower, announced to P., who was still asleep and whose dreams would no doubt be visited by visions of horror, that I was returning to the scene of the crime.

When I got out of the car, I was amazed by the stillness of the scene. The birds had been up for a long time, but I could hear only two crows calling to each other in the distance. Even the river, its rushing waters normally audible from the wayside cross, seemed to have gone silent. I walked over to the little bridge to confirm that, in spite of the summer's abundant rain, the river had lost its energy. The banks that had been flooded in spring were lined with rocks of all sizes piled up there by thousands of spiral swellings, and the height of the water had dropped at least a metre. I picked up a stone and hurled it into the pool at the bottom of the bridge, which had largely dried up over the course of the summer and was no longer a pool in anything but name. It hit the thin layer of water stagnating on the silty bottom with a muffled noise before sinking into the mud beside a heap of stones that other people had probably tossed in before me to break the dense silence.

The anemic flow of water, like the still of the morning, told me fall was on the way, and that if I didn't want to forestall Heather once more and have to observe her from the January snows, I'd need to get a move on. I walked back to the cross, the site where the photo of Heather, Vince, and Jackson had been taken, and where Heather had parked her father's Buick before she disappeared. Then I walked around in an effort to recreate the scene and bring together the various factors of which I was aware.

From where I was standing, I could no longer see Jackson, who was hidden by the front of the Buick, though I could just about see Vince's head and shoulders as he smiled at an invisible dog. Heather, however, I could see more clearly. She wasn't smiling anymore, and was struggling, against time's grip or the constraints of the image, to rush toward Jackson and pick up his inert body from where it lay in front of the Buick. In the background, at the mouth of the logging road that joins La Languette immediately beyond the bridge, two snowmobilers were watching a distressed Heather leaning over the lifeless dog and sobbing, *Jackson, Jackson, my love*, before she turned around to face the two snowmobilers and yelled, *Don't come near my dog, you fucking maniacs, don't you ever come near him again.* Then she ran toward them to slap them, kick them, and spit in their faces. I was about to go lend a hand when the noise of a horn made me start and I realized I was standing in the middle of the road, fighting the shadows that had swallowed up Heather Thorne.

Embarrassed, I retreated to the edge of the roadside ditch to allow the vehicle to pass. In it were a red-haired man, Herb McMillan, and a burlier guy, Gilles Ferland, who were driving very slowly and staring at me as if they'd seen an apparition as they passed. I watched as their eyes widened, their mouths opened, and Ferland murmured *tabarnak* before McMillan stepped on the gas and the truck sped away in a cloud of dust. When the dust settled, I ran to my car, and near it I noticed the shadow of R. putting his camera back into a leather case and smiling at Heather, radiant in the newborn day.

P. was finishing breakfast when I got back. I said a quick hello and went straight to the bathroom to look in the mirror. A few sweat-drenched locks of hair covered my forehead, and I pushed them back so I could see the whole of my face, which, it seemed to me, was retreating into the mirror, beyond the reach of my outstretched hands, moving further and further away, pushed by some force that wanted to destroy it or ruin it.

I jumped when P., his broad shape framed in the doorway, asked me what was going on. I tried to answer, but the mirror had taken my voice as well, then my face disappeared over there, in the tempestuous winds of winter 1980.

Herb McMillan and Gilles Ferland hadn't been dreaming. They really had seen Heather Thorne's ghost in La Languette, come back to haunt the location of her unhappiness and their crime. I wiped my forehead, now covered in snow, and moved away from the mirror, aware that the hand holding the pen would soon be nothing more than the scrawny, evanescent hand of a woman returned from among the dead.

There are fewer and fewer moths, and the large-winged kinds have been replaced by small moths, long and boring, whose names I don't know, and which might, for all I know, not even be moths, but insects that have failed in their attempt to live by flying. Three or four of them followed me into my study after my usual evening walk and, not content with hurling themselves at the inside of the lamp, they swoop at me, clinging to my hair, fluttering against my forehead, and then fly back to the lamp with their wings beating erratically. Even the cat isn't bothered by them. He twitches his ears and tail whenever one of them brushes against his fur, and then sinks back into his dreams, which I can tell are as agitated as my thoughts, all focused on McMillan, Ferland, and R., who are perhaps plotting right now, huddled over the wooden bridge spanning the slow river.

Did I make it all up this morning, or did I just invent what was necessary for my autumn to superimpose itself over Heather's, and for us to see our last snowfalls together? Did I invent the mirror or did it invent me? Did I invent Jackson's death and Heather's tears, did I invent the men who saw my ghost, my double, the shadow side of my soul?

My questions hang suspended in the smoky room and I am no longer trying to answer them, because how would I know, when the rain touches my skin, if I am writing what *is* or am becoming what is written?

The days are shortening imperceptibly, one or two minutes at a time, and here we are back again at that time of year where I have to cover the east-facing windows in my study if I don't want to be blinded by the light skimming past the tops of the spruces.

Shadows form on the curtain, shapes so distinct they occasionally frighten me, and whose contours I try to sharpen, telling myself they're probably just intimations of wandering souls surrounding the house, spirits of the place whose desire to be seen sometimes projects them onto the curtain where I make the ink flow, joining the sun so that their transparent matter is imprinted on the supple fabric.

P. has gone to the city to do some research, and to take part in a conference on eco-criticism — a word in which I hear echoes of mountains inhabited by animals mocking our desperation to understand nature when, instead, we should simply allow it to act upon the course of our lives.

It's the first time since we moved into this house that I've been alone in it. The solace of my solitude enhances the peace of where we are, and I try to enjoy these days without words rendering my voice hoarse, and aim to rediscover the silence free of human noise that has been my natural environment for years.

In the chair I'm sitting in, all I can hear is the wind's whistling and the gentle snoring of the cat sleeping beside me. I won't work this evening, I'll just listen to the creaking house and then go to bed.

A hand has just knocked on the window of my bedroom on the second floor, the hand of a woman in distress calling, *Help me, for Christ's sake.* I don't know if it's Heather, Sissy Morgan, Elisabeth Mulligan, or one of the other characters who've pleaded for sympathy over the years, and I'm not all that bothered about finding out, since the absurd fear of hearing a voice in the bedroom next door has kept me awake ever since a rustling of fabric dragged me from the numbness into which we are plunged by the fleeting images we experience before sleep. I was swimming in the cloudy waters of a mountain lake when I heard the sound of fabric being rubbed between two hands. I sat bolt upright in bed, my heart beating, alarmed by the feeling of a vague but real threat weighing on the silence of the house.

I've not moved since then, because I'm almost certain that as soon as I drop my guard, P.'s voice — even though P. isn't here — will pipe up behind the partition separating our two bedrooms to wish me "Goodnight, honey, goodnight," due to some phenomenon reproducing sounds after their echo has faded, as if their effect were so imprinted by their regular enunciation that they repeated by themselves, or perhaps because, quite simply, the fear of fear sometimes has us imagine all the possible and familiar resonances of horror at its most intimate. Given all this, the woman whose nails are scratching my windowpanes is just one bad dream among many.

Dawn finally came, the pink at the horizon illuminating motionless clouds. There's no mark on the window from the scratching nails, P.'s bedroom breathes the cold air of empty spaces, and the cat is calm, completely untroubled by the ghostly presences that amount to nothing but my own anxiety.

I make myself a strong coffee and sit down at my desk, where more concrete problems than those disturbing me during the night await. Who killed Jackson, and what did Heather know about the accident? These are the questions I need to answer if I am to establish whether I imagined the scene I witnessed at La Languette — Heather angrily screaming at Ferland and McMillan, *Don't come near my dog, you fucking maniacs* — or if this was just me projecting from a past whose violence still permeates the countryside if you look at it from a certain angle, just as the echoes of certain voices can also be found in it.

The simplest solution would be to ask Heather, but I'm afraid she'd be waiting for me with her gun and would terminate me before the final scene. In any case, I feel as though I lost contact with her the moment I entrusted Vince with the task of making her live again for me, and particularly since I understood Howard W. Thorne was still contemplating schemes of revenge beside a tombstone under which a body lies that I dare not exhume to compare its features with my own.

I have pushed Heather toward inertia and am unable, now, to think of her as anything but pale and trembling in the middle of the endless autumn, engulfed by leaves turned red and falling unceasingly among trees offering up their bare trunks to the cold. I have to get her out of there, must absolutely get her out of there before the mould that has attacked the seats of her Buick starts to make blemishes on her skin.

———

Meanwhile, Heather dreams of a sea she has never known; of unfurling foamy waves submerging the rocks at the edge of the beach in a spectacular roaring, their din increasing as the waves come in, they'll soon be where she is, inundating the forest and tipping over the car we'll watch drifting with the docks toward the dried-up rivers.

For P.'s homecoming I've prepared a herb omelette, a green salad, and an apple pie—my "famous apple pie," as I call it—made with the fruit of the apple tree that leans by the fence whose rails we'll need to move if we don't want the tree's lower branches to be damaged. And I've opened a bottle of the Ardèche wine P. really likes, no doubt due to his memories of the region, good memories, somewhat darkened by the death of his friend from there.

He proposes a toast to the dead friend and I propose another to all our dead loved ones, because they are increasingly numerous, because we live right at the heart of a zone slowly depopulating to the rhythm of passing seasons that break our bones. Then he tells me about his trip, about the finds he made in certain bookstores and the stench of the city, its dense, heavy air, before asking me how I spent my solitary days. I don't have much to tell him, because solitude is silent, and I have no intention of telling him about the voice in the night, *Good night, honey, good night* . . . So I tell him how Heather climbed onto the roof so she could scratch at my window, adding that she might be dead right now as we're drinking the Ardèche wine, drowned by the fury of an unknown sea and lengthening the list of our dead loved ones.

P. says no, she can't be dead because I look more and more like her every day. "Your hair," he says, "the paleness of your skin," which he touches with his fingertips. Then the sun goes down and we go to bed. When I turn out my lamp, I hear his voice on the other side of the partition wishing me "Goodnight, honey, goodnight," and a shiver runs through my sweat-drenched body.

Vince doesn't know how Jackson died. All he knows is that Jackson was run over by a vehicle, that Heather cried for a week before she disappeared in La Languette, and that he barely saw her during this time, barely talked to her, because she was constantly shouting or murmuring, "Jackson, Jackson, my love." Nothing else, just these shouts and murmurs, a troubling anger. "I don't know anything else, what do you want me to say?"

When he stops he is out of breath, and I can hear the tick-tock of the clock on the old stove, which emits a kind of trill when the second hand passes the 12. I abandon him to this preoccupying noise, my coffee already cold on the linen placemat.

I have to get Heather out of the woods. I have to get Heather out of the woods. I pound the desk as I wrack my brains, unable to figure out how to change the impetus of Heather's situation, and all the while Vince is surrounded by the haunting tick-tocking of the clock; he lowers his head, eyes too heavy to contemplate the future and tells me I need to move fast.

It's impossible for Heather to be dead, P. has confirmed. It's impossible that she doesn't exist, because the phenomenon of sympathetic assimilation, where one person takes on another person's features and vice versa, requires two people. What he forgot to add is that at the end of the process — when the assimilation has evolved to the point where they are mistaken for each other — one of the two has to retreat and let the other one take over. Will it be Heather or me who quits the stage before the curtain falls?

VII.

In time, the repetition of events ends by drawing, in its wake, shapes traced with such persistence that we are able to deduce a few truths about the motive determining this repetition.

I step on the gas, a woman with a young and mellifluous voice utters the word *glorious*, metal crunches and crumples so resoundingly it brings to mind the terror of the final straight, the atmosphere inside the car is suffocating, and I fall into a red abyss.

It's time to rewrite Heather Thorne's autumn.

The phosphorescent clock on the dashboard shows quarter after midnight when Heather Thorne regains consciousness. It takes her a few minutes to orient herself: the car skidding for no reason, her acceleration into the woods, the final impact, the irrevocable cracking of the branches, the metallic crumpling sounds, and then the red silence of fainting.

She touches the blood flowing over her left temple with her fingertips and looks in the glove compartment for something to clean up with, but all she finds is a pile of Led Zeppelin, Neil Young, and Steve Earle CDs. Then she manages to grab her bag from the back seat despite the searing pain ripping through her right thigh. She takes out a silk scarf and knots it firmly around her leg, presses a few tissues to her temple, and then swallows a couple of ibuprofen tablets that lodge in her throat. Water . . . she would love some water.

She tries to open the car door but it's jammed and blocked by a tree trunk. With difficulty, she slides over to the passenger seat, lifting her legs over the gear stick with an effort that forces a cry of pain out of her, but the door on that side also refuses to open, which is when she spots the glimmering axe on the back seat. She picks it up and smashes the glass of the window with the tool's wide end. Shards of glass hook into her hair and she uses the sleeve of her leather jacket to break the pieces remaining in haphazard relief on the frame. She will have a few wounds on her hands and wrists, but they'll disappear or scar over in the coming days, and the right sleeve of her jacket will also retain marks, like animal scratches, from this incident.

Finally, she extricates herself from the vehicle and takes in great gulps of the night air, her breaths turning into gasps. Water . . . she needs to find some water. She crawls forward, her right leg useless, looking for any reflection of the light of the three-quarter moon shining through the branches, and then she notices a slope. There must be water down there. She lets herself roll down the incline, unable to suppress the cries of pain burning her throat, and ends up near the thin trickle of a stream snaking through the moss. She plunges her face in and drinks until she is no longer thirsty, and then stretches out on the bed of moss, out of breath but with her thirst slaked.

Stars are shining above the tops of the trees, and she has no idea where she is, who she is, or why she has ended up in this forest. She remembers nothing but the irrepressible force pressing her foot down on the accelerator—and then the image of a woman appears in her memory, a woman standing by the side of the road, her arms half raised, and then words as vivid as the pain searing through her right thigh come into her mind: *My name must be Andrée, her name must be Andrée. We are hunted women.*

I heard the nasal cries of a flock of geese I could not see crossing the sky. Winter will be here soon.

"My name must be Andrée, Andrée A.," Heather says beneath her breath as the mud she's applied to her wounds sets and bits of dry earth with perfectly straight edges fall off her injured thigh.

My name must be Andrée, she thinks, the name evoking for her nothing but the distressed expression of a woman raising her arms near a stream with a background of sparklingly colourful coniferous and deciduous forest in the background.

My name must be Andrée, she insists — *Andrée A.* — before the muffled din of metal rubbing against the bark flying in dusty fragments around the Buick brings her back to reality, and she corrects herself: *My name must be Andrée, Andrée A. But I am not who I think I am.*

As is my habit every Wednesday afternoon, I visited my mother in the nursing home with the endless turquoise walls where she has been compelled to retire since her last stay in the hospital. The pair of women I've dubbed the "two sad sisters" are sitting in the living room, in the same spot as usual, mute and staring at nothing except their own disappearing past. The younger one's head is resting on the other woman's shoulder, hours spent in silence. A light sometimes appears in the younger one's eyes as someone approaches, but then extinguishes itself quickly, not strong enough to reach the nearly blind eyes of the other. Hours spent in silence waiting for lunch, dinner, night.

I walk past them with my mother, whom I'm taking outside for a breath of fresh air. The younger one's eyes had responded for a moment when I greeted her, but then her head fell back onto the other one's shoulder as the door clicked shut.

With my mother at my side, I gazed at life — at wasps, grasshoppers, yellow September butterflies, at the heavy bunches of ripening grapes weighing down the Virginia creeper that runs the length of the big porch, at birds, children—*yes, life*—but the sad sisters followed me home and here they are in a corner of my study, the younger one's head resting on the other one's shoulder, motionless and silent though perhaps communicating with their thoughts or in the short sighing breaths of their boredom, two broken dolls bringing to mind the dead twins that haunt the corridors of the Overlook Hotel in Stanley Kubrick's *The Shining*, a film that made a great impression on me; two sad sisters who look more like each other with each passing day, due to that phenomenon by which one person absorbs another's sadness and vice versa.

Last night, as I was getting ready for bed, someone knocked on our front door. "Heather!" I exclaimed, my heart beating fast, because ever since the moment when I realized it was imperative that I get her out of the woods, I've had the feeling she's been moving further away instead of closer, and that the day will come when I'll no longer be able to catch her at all.

I approached the door but stepped back a little when I saw a woman I didn't know on the porch—black hair, on the short side—and a teenager, her son, who was almost a head taller than her. I was wary of opening the door to them, strangers who show up in the middle of the night usually bringing only bad news, but since the woman had seen me I didn't have much of a choice.

The diminutive woman entered first, and then the son, to tell us they'd just hit a deer with their vehicle, that the son's phone wasn't working, and they wanted to call the police. *This is just a smokescreen*, I thought initially, *these people want something else, the father is probably hiding behind the cedars with the older son, ready to rush into the house as soon as his wife gives the agreed signal, maybe smoothing her hair over her forehead, as she is doing right now.*

Convinced I'd seen through their plot, I quickly went back to the window, where all I could make out was my worried reflection, then that of the small woman, whose wide eyes betrayed a curious terror. I apologized, a little ashamed of my reaction. "A shadow," I said, as the little woman started to squint, her dark eyes staring at me with a kind of rat-like nervousness that reminded me of the way a rat's eyes dart around as it notes the crumbs on the floor, noises in the walls, and hostile smells, making me uncomfortable. The little woman was afraid, perhaps asking herself just who were these strangers whose door she and her son had knocked on, because you never really know whom you'll encounter, it could easily be someone bad, and you might think the smiling people opening their door to you are there to help when really they have just one idea in mind: to seize the day and give their murderous impulses free rein.

The small woman's fear was that of Little Red Riding Hood when she innocently steps into the mouth of the wolf—only how could we be the wolf? I swept away the horrors intruding on my mind, wild beasts salivating over fresh meat, the screams of the prey, the silence, broken only by the sound of lapping mouths that follows their execution, doing my best to convince myself this woman's manner was nothing like the nervousness of the wretched little hoodlum who goes into the house of a couple of frail old people, intent on stealing their meagre possessions. Besides, people who show up in the middle of the night to rob and, if necessary, flay you, tend to be calm and cold, sizing up the situation in a single glance, noting the exits, the weapons, telling a joke as they measure up the strength of all the people present and then stabbing you or tying you up as soon as you turn your back or show any sign of weakness.

P., who did not share my unease, invited the small woman and her son to sit down as I dialled the police and then held out the phone to the woman, who'd taken off her shoes on the carpet, and whose feet I couldn't help staring at, the toes spaced too far apart, a wide gap between the big toe and the next one. As I did so, the woman was answering the police's questions — no, the deer didn't die on the road, it collapsed on the shoulder, yes, her car was totalled, but she had insurance, at least she thought she did, she wasn't sure anymore, the accident had shaken her. After she hung up, she stared vaguely in the direction of my study, as if she no longer knew where she was. Then she and her son thanked us and left.

Standing at the threshold, I watched them disappear beyond the arch and into the darkness. I imagined the mother deer, who might not have been killed, who was perhaps dying in the ditch, fear in her stomach, worrying about her little ones. "I knew it," I said to P., "I knew those two would bring bad news, it was written in their eyes, in that woman's posture, in the way her neck hunched into her shoulders and made her look even shorter next to her son."

"It was written," I repeated a couple of times as Holy Crappy Owl, who'd not said a word for ages, wiggled at the end of his string to screech, "It was written, it was written, it was written . . ." I calmed him down before he strangled himself, and left the house, thinking I might be able to find the doe and relieve her suffering, but I wasn't brave enough for that, not incensed enough to stick the knife P. gave me into her throat, the Smith & Wesson Special Tactical with the black serrated blade, so I turned around and went home, not proud of myself for being such a scaredy cat. I sent up a prayer to the god of deer, assuring myself that, despite the cruelty we attribute to it, nature can be compassionate and kill quickly — with a single blow — all this before the deer has the time to realize she's on her way, or to worry about her little ones who will bleat like calves, exactly like calves.

The big-game hunting season is coming. People are already allowed to kill with a bow or a crossbow, but soon we'll be hearing gunshots and seeing bodies strapped to the tops of cars, legs tied, hooves in the air, or sticking out of the backs of trucks. Right about now Gilles Ferland and Herb McMillan must be getting their ammunition ready, cleaning their guns and anticipating the first stage of the hunt — unless, that is, they're now incapable of killing, even a fly, even a mouse, gripped by nausea as soon as they hear an animal's cry, as soon as they imagine its blood on the rotten floor of the cellar. I don't know. These men are brutes. Not sure if you can make a brute into a decent guy. I don't believe so.

P. went out with his walking stick and flannel shirt with the aim of finding the doe, who'd apparently been struck about two hundred metres from the house. "No doe," he muttered when he came back. Then he went to his study.

I stayed frozen in place, my pen in the air, in the middle of a sentence describing the found doe. Could I have been right last night, when I imagined the father and the older son behind the cedars, and that the operation was aborted for some reason of which I was unaware? Could the mother and son have been on a reconnaissance mission while the father and the other son were waiting in a car that wasn't the slightest bit wrecked? Were they doing so in case things turned out badly, in case the people who opened the door to the wife and youngest son were crazy, maniacal psychopaths?

I wonder again about the woman's jitters; perhaps the husband had ignored her qualms and forced her to implement his plan, and she couldn't help but be afraid of the consequences of her actions. Unless someone had picked up the deer. The father, for example, returning with his two sons, or the policeman who'd answered my call, or maybe the men the police officer sent along—his uncle and brother-in-law—for the still-fresh meat.

I have no idea what really happened, but I'm keeping an

eye out. If the little woman shows up again, I'll make her spill the beans and ask her what they did with the meat, the gun, why her husband was waiting outside, behind the trees or in the car, with the elder son, the brute of the family ready to slit throats for just a few measly dollars.

Sitting down near the stream, Heather breathes in the fall scents perfuming the forest. The smells soothe her, though she doesn't exactly know why, and make her want to walk until she loses herself, until she's no more than an animal sniffing the wind. She imagines this animal, half horse, half deer, galloping freely into a clearing, its hooves stirring up the brown grass that the autumn has flattened to the ground, its nose sniffing at the fireweed fluff, before a scent of snow tickles its nostrils, leading it to panic and snort, sensing the quiet threat that northern winters bring.

"No, not that, not snow," says Heather quietly, halted by the new scent in the wind, her memory absorbed by a blizzard that whipped her skin till it was red and the roar of the snowmobiles that once chased her. *Gun*, she thinks, *gun*, *quick*, and she struggles back up the slope, catching her breath as she moves level with the carpet of dead leaves, before finally making her way back to the spot where the Buick stopped, its path blocked by the mass of trees.

Vigilantly looking around, she supports herself on a branch and opens the Buick's trunk, which squeaks like an old rusty door. Lying on the worn carpet in the back of it gleams the gun she expected to find. Not far away, the blade of the axe she dropped as she made her way out of the car sparkles amid the shards of glass.

I was right. So was Holy Crappy Owl. The little woman isn't innocent. She came here as a scout, to spy on me and gather information about Heather Thorne, about how I live, about the set-up of the house. She also used the opportunity to note the arrangement of my study, which she could see out of the corner of her glazed eye as she was sitting at the kitchen table.

As for the son, he's not the innocent victim of a cunning mother. He, too, is in it up to his neck, pushed into it by the brute of an older brother for whom he feels limitless admiration. I never should have opened up my house to this teenager looking too ordinary to be true, nor to that woman with the too-widely spaced toes, who probably saw the shadow of the bombyx on my desk and my manuscript, open to page 102 and the scene where Heather writes the note implicating Ferland and McMillan.

I was in the Canadian Tire of the town nearest to me that afternoon, shopping for new windshield wipers. Since I was already there, I decided to buy some of the hardware we needed to strengthen the fences, you can never have too much. I was putting it all in my cart when I noticed them—the woman and the son—in the hunting-equipment aisle. They were accompanied by Gilles Ferland, who likely did still hunt as he had a camo jacket in his cart, as well as a decoy for calling moose and a few other items plainly indicating that he didn't plan to spend the fall sitting in his living room.

I slipped into a side aisle so they wouldn't notice me and wondered what I should do. And that was when the small woman walked past the end of my aisle with her son, recognized me, and dodged away. I needed to catch up with her before she disappeared so I could be sure that Ferland was real. I noticed her heading toward the exit. She was shod in tall, dirty boots, like the kind you wear fishing, but I couldn't help seeing the outline of her toes under the rubber, the toes of devils, hypocrites, and liars.

"Mrs. Ferland!" I shouted as she passed through the closing doors. Hearing my voice, she turned around sharply, grabbed her son by the arm and dragged him into the parking lot. By the time I was outside, a red truck was squealing its tires on the wet asphalt.

This incident happened a few hours ago and I'm still in shock. I repeat to Holy Crappy Owl that he was right, that we were taken in, and Holy waggles, "I told you so, I told you so, it was written," as the two sad sisters go to sleep in a corner of my study, the head of one resting on the other's shoulder, and P. snores on the second floor, unaware that he was also deceived and now I am a genuine danger to him.

Heather frantically munches her way through the few pistachios remaining in the bottom of the container she always keeps in her car. The phosphorescent clock on the dashboard tells her she's been there for around six hours, which is confirmed by the light slowly brightening the sky, but she's convinced that she's been in the clearing a lot longer than that, that young tree shoots will soon poke their way through the Buick's floor to lick at the windshield and surface through the rusty roof, and that the place she's in is not unknown to her, and it's possible that the clock has shown 6:15 numerous times since the accident, even if her thigh is not yet healed, even if her scratches are still bleeding. Her knowledge of the surrounding area is far too intimate for her to have only spent one night there.

She gets out of the car and sits down beside a pine tree, the gun between her legs and the axe by her side, wondering just what she should do: wait for her suspected assailant, or look for somewhere to take shelter? But where can a woman with no idea who she is, or where she comes from, find shelter? She clings to the few words that might give her some semblance of identity: "My name must be Andrée, Andrée A. I'm an injured woman, fleeing."

Repeating the words, she tries to view them from without and to see herself as separate from the words and not one entity with them. She strives to anchor herself in some sort of reality, but can't make out her body, her face—still can't see her face, even though she's spent ages staring into the side mirror of the car, which broke from the impact of the accident and is dangling down the door: blue eyes, the iris encircled with yellow; fine, mid-length hair, naturally wavy; pale lips, and a high forehead partly hidden by uneven bangs. But all this is getting muddled, the lips are stretching out or thickening, the nose is lengthening, the face is becoming a mask, a caricature.

"*Jesus*," she spits out suddenly, which teaches her something else: she's an injured woman who swears when things go wrong. And things are definitely going wrong, very badly wrong. Her injured leg is preventing her from concentrating and representing herself clearly in the world: me, me, maybe Andrée, lost, Andrée A. She doesn't know what the A stands for; for indecision, maybe, or to feminize a name whose gender is determined by a silent vowel.

As for her surname, she doesn't even know its first letter. But she feels that her father is close by, in this forest that will soon reveal her real name to her. She can sense his presence in the smells around her, in the sun warming her feet shod in heavy boots, men's boots, made for walking far away from the noise of inhabited places, but which are currently no use whatsoever because of the wounded leg that will force her to crawl if she decides to leave, or to improvise crutches or a cane with broken branches. But it is becoming increasingly clear that she won't leave, or at least not before she is certain that, wherever she goes, she'll be able to confront the men who hunted her down. Her memory is empty but alert. She can sense the attackers' imminent arrival.

How could I not have recognized Ferland's wife, who challenged me with her weary gaze on the day before Christmas Eve from her living room window? Despite the distance, I observed the oval of her face, the blackness of her dyed hair, how much smaller she was than her sons. I'd seen her hand grip the younger boy's shoulder, move a stray lock away from her forehead, but I didn't put it all together.

Gloria Ferland, as I will call her now for expediency's sake — and because it's impossible to separate her from Gilles, her dreadful husband — Gloria Ferland is one of those women whose face you forget as soon as you turn away, its evasive and empty eyes, too unremarkable for the memory of them to stick, the ordinary lips. Hers is a mask that dissolves when other people aren't looking and disappears when the door closes on its banality. Gloria Ferland is the sort of person only distinguished by some lack in their physiognomy which, most often hidden, defines their entire identity.

Unsettled by this observation, I wake up Holy Crappy Owl to tell him the little woman is called Gloria, and that you have to see her feet to understand her true nature. Crappy, barely emerged from the universe of his mad dreams, immediately snorts with laughter. "Gloria! Gloria! Gloria!" he screeches before intoning a song of his own invention about Gloria's feet.

VIII.

I didn't invent Gloria Ferland, nor did I wish for her to show up in my daily life, an appearance more accurately described as an intrusion, given the events that followed. I simply opened my door to her — and, along with her, somebody else I'd not created, a man who came into my house, poking and prying into all the objects around us, adding his own smell to the suddenly sinister atmosphere of the place, his marks on the wooden doors, and his prints on the furniture, embedded beneath the surface.

The man's trespassing, which surreptitiously violated the house to its very foundations, which stirred up the dust on the crumbling ground, has tipped the story into a world of back roads populated by crooks. This novel doesn't belong to me anymore.

December 2, 2015. I've just finished typing up my manuscript, word by word, sentence by sentence, page after page, going back through the seasons, reliving my moods, feeling once more the strange sensation of seeing a woman who could only be me at the wheel of a Buick driving toward dusk, and all this because, a few weeks ago, when P. and I were out just for a short time, the house was burgled.

It was Thanksgiving Monday, the geese who'd managed to escape the hunters' bullets were heading south, the sun was shining, and the sparrows singing. It was one of those days when it seemed nothing disagreeable could happen, and the car sped toward our house without my having any morbid thoughts at all about the final straight. Next to me, P. was humming an old blues tune and beating time on the dashboard. Everything seemed right with the world.

As we approached the house, we noticed a blue vehicle driving out of the yard, not new, a pickup truck, but we weren't really paying much attention because a lot of people turn around in our driveway due to the reassuring juxtaposition of seasons in front of and behind the arch. But I saw the guy's face clearly, the driver with his bandit's mouth, black glasses, goatee, and mid-length slightly curly hair that obviously hadn't been brushed in some time. I stared straight at the dark lenses, and, as his appearance was not familiar, I forgot about it, decided I did not know the man.

It was only when we'd gone inside and set our bags of groceries down on the table that we noticed the basement door had been smashed open. In that same moment the elder son came to mind, and I raced into my study to find that my computer had disappeared, as well as my hard drive and an old computer I kept in the drawer. P., who had rushed to his study, shouted out that his computer had also been stolen, as well as his binoculars and the fake gun he'd purchased years before when he was considering writing a gangster story.

I wanted to set off in pursuit of the blue vehicle, like a fearless and irreproachable heroine — a woman who wouldn't let anyone give her trouble, a cop in a Raymond Chandler story — but P. held me back. The guy was long gone and no doubt hiding in a barn, in a garage, or along the lane to the cabin. So instead we telephoned the real police, but they couldn't do much either, what with our having been too stupid to note down the vehicle's licence plate, at least that's what the young policeman sitting at the kitchen table must have been thinking, sitting where the small woman had, though he'd not taken off his boots. Police officers never take their boots off, it would make them too vulnerable, and I couldn't see his toes.

He didn't treat us like imbeciles, he was too polite for

that. I would even say he was kind, he was nice, laughing
at the dull jokes of a woman on the verge of a nervous
breakdown. But he must have thought it, if only because
everybody else thought it — that's to say, P., me, Crappy,
and the cats, who, luckily, were outside when the brute
smashed down our two basement doors, an external one
and then another leading up to the main floor, because
you never know when bastards like that are going to show
up with their dark glasses, goatees, and mouths that don't
laugh. If he'd touched the cats, I'd have killed him, I'd
have tracked him all the way to the Amazon and turned
into a vigilante, a character right out of a trashy novel,
someone not nice at all, who doesn't flinch away from
anything and who's not afraid of drawing her gun or
unsheathing her knife, nor afraid to have blood spurt on
her old-fashioned leather jacket.

But the calico was in the woods when we got back —
probably under the wild roses growing on the other side
of the old fence — and the first cat was hiding behind the
cedars, near the ditch claimed by indigenous vegetation.
He'd come to meet me as soon as I was out of the car
to tell me what he'd seen. He'd witnessed the elder son
breaking into the house and was trying to explain what
had happened, but I didn't understand his meowing, his
tetchiness, the indignation of a cat whose territory has
been invaded by a crook.

I'd come inside with P., a bag of groceries in each hand,
and seen the basement door, with its latch flown right over
to the shelf where we keep our gloves, mittens, penknives,

compasses. I'd seen, beneath the cast-iron stove, the tray of cat grass that the thief knocked over when the latch gave way, and then the reproduction *Manneken-Pis* sculpture with the penis in the shape of corkscrew, a hideous thing, that was knocked over as well. And then I noticed that my computer was no longer on my desk. My heart started to race and then slowed down dangerously, to such an extent that I leaned on the table so as not to collapse among the white sheets of paper flying around me like the white laundry you see hanging outside on a spring day. That carried on for one or two minutes: red, white, red, white, until I grabbed the phone and dialled 911.

I've just finished retyping my manuscript, a copy of which I've put in a safe place whose location I will only reveal under torture. But this doesn't really solve my problem, because if my suspicions are correct, then my novel is now in the hands of Gloria Ferland, and she's probably read it to her husband Gilles, who, has in turn no doubt passed it on to Herb McMillan during the time I took to type it out again and alter a few details — just tiny things, because it's pointless trying to backtrack when a text is already out in the world. Once it's written, it's written, and Holy Crappy Owl is telling me I'm in a big mess here.

The elder of the two sad sisters was carried off by sorrow, may she rest in peace, but her shadow is still there in a corner of my study with the shadows of the bombyx and the wandering souls sketching themselves on the curtains. She'll also be present in the living room of the building with endless turquoise walls, still sitting in the same place, motionless and silent and with the younger sister's head lightly resting upon her shoulder; and the younger sister will also be motionless and silent, remembering the warmth of a living body, eyes now riveted on its absence, on the dreadful void of turquoise days.

While death was going about its business in the house of the sad sisters, Heather gathered branches to place in an open space near the Buick and then surround them with stones, some — the most beautiful ones — white, others grey, with the aim of lighting a fire, because the nights were getting colder despite the seeming inertia of time, and their dampness was penetrating her leather jacket, no longer enough to keep her warm. She knows that the fire might attract the very people she's afraid of and alert them to her position, but she has no choice if she is to remain on guard and not succumb to the numbing effect of the cold. And she does still have her gun, her axe, and her determination — the desire to make it through the autumn augmenting her strength.

She strikes one of the matches she finds at the bottom of her bag and cups her hands around it so that it doesn't go out, because after this one she only has eleven matches left: eleven nights of fire. Then she huddles over the twigs she's slipped among the branches, catching the flame one after another and communicating their heat to the smallest branches as they also start to catch, and Heather can breathe at last. She backs up, leans against the car, and will wait for tomorrow, unless the cold brings snow, because she's afraid the two men will be able to track her scent in a northeast wind, in which case another day in this place would be impossible.

Vince has piled a load of dead leaves into a big metal barrel covered with a grill, and you can see the smoke of the fire blazing in the barrel from the road. As I get out of my car, a sudden gust of wind blows the smoke in my direction, and all I can see are the glowing embers at the bottom of the barrel through the tiny gaps in the metal.

I skirt around the smoke and go over to Vince, who's waiting for the fire to die down a little before he adds to the barrel the branches affected by Cherry Black Knot disease he cut the day before. His eyes are red from the smoke and he has a large stripe of soot on his left cheek, like a long scar emphasizing the pallor of his face. He invites me to sit down on a log, hands me a cigarette, and amid the crackling of the leaves and the branches, we smoke in silence.

We're both aware that, from this point on, we are linked by the silent violence that carried Heather Waverley to her grave, and that the situation in which we find ourselves might just prompt the right words to allow us to penetrate the secrets surrounding her death. We'll talk soon enough, when the fire can safely go out without our watching it and we go inside into the warm, because the wind that was just starting up when I arrived has become stronger, a south wind piercing our clothes and probably bringing on bad weather. For Vince too, there is nothing good in this wind, so he throws sand on the embers and decides he'll burn what's left of the leaves and branches tomorrow.

Inside, our clothes smell strongly of fall smoke, and I bury my nose in my scarf, reviving the memory of a few dozen falls gone by that were also redolent of woodsmoke, as the bitter aroma of the coffee Vince is brewing mingles with the cinder perfume.

Just as Vince takes a seat opposite mine at the table, R. appears in the kitchen, bringing fall scents with him too. Vince offers his brother a coffee, but R. pretends that he has to go out right away, that he needs to cord wood at his house. Neither Vince nor I are fooled: R. is simply unable to breathe the same air as me. But finally I'm ready to confront his animosity, because there are too many unresolved questions between us, too many grey areas in which the shadow of Gilles Ferland's face can be discerned. I tell him, "I won't bite, Réal," speaking his name for the first time since we met at Vince's, and this unsettles him slightly, though not enough for him to accept Vince's coffee. He lowers his head and opens the door to go back to where he came from, to the void he evaporates into every time he leaves Vince's house.

"She said she won't bite you," mutters Vince, clenching his fists, and Réal stops in the doorway, surprised by his palpable anger. "Sit down for a couple minutes," he orders, and Réal reluctantly comes and sits down to my left, at the far end of the table. The silence weighs heavily for a few moments, as loaded as Vince's anger, and I jump right in and ask Réal what he knows of Gilles Ferland, whom I saw here with him a few weeks earlier, how long they've known each other, if he has a snowmobile and if he hunts in La Languette, but Réal's face closes up with each of my questions and eventually he pushes his chair back violently and tells me to leave Ferland in peace, that the past is the past and we can't change it.

Ten seconds later the door slams, but Réal has revealed enough for me to know that Gilles Ferland's life is one of troubled secrets that provoke rage when some stranger, who has by chance shown up in the survivor's guilty present, desperately scratches the ground in an attempt to exhume them.

The south wind did bring snow, and Réal Morissette, propelled by a cocktail of anger and despair, strode through the blizzard ripping at the La Languette trees with a yowling that could have been mistaken for the wailing of an animal in heat.

His face red from the driving snow, Réal followed the track of the myriad paths he'd taken a thousand times, familiar with every landmark, every fork, every rise and fall, remembering he'd killed a deer at the bottom of that slope, or this stream where he'd taken off his boots one spring evening to relieve his hurting feet in the icy water, or to quench his thirst on a blazing hot day. But the succour of these places in which he could usually find solace reminded him that there is no peace for a man whose conscience is burdened with a lie.

At the junction of two paths, he turns right, hoping to lose himself and then, in his gut, he experiences the mounting, paralytic fear of someone who suddenly realizes all the trees look the same, the stumps and mounds too, who realizes his footsteps have disappeared behind him and that he risks wandering even deeper in, where nobody will ever find him again. And yet Réal Morissette knows the forest too well to be lost, even after walking for several more hours and well away from the roads dissecting the territory.

Tired of fighting the pain tearing him apart, he heads north and ends up in a clearing swept by powdery snow whirling in spirals, trying to breach the wall of trees but being pushed back into the centre of the clearing, where the snow again lifts up in the spirals that the old folk around here associate with witchcraft. He moves on through the blowing snow, lifts his arms to the sky and pleads with the devil to take him, but the witches are the ones whipping him, whistling with the wind right into the heart of his cries. At the end of his strength, he eventually lets himself slide down the trunk of a damn tree and, through his tears, mutters the name of a deceased young girl: Heather, Heather Waverley.

The snow took Heather by surprise, and in vain she blows on the twigs, which blaze up briefly before breaking up and falling through the criss-crossed branches.

The phosphorescent clock on the dashboard shows only a quarter after four and night is already falling, a night that will be long and sleepless. Making the most of the last rays of the setting sun, Heather picks up the axe with the intention of cutting a few pine branches to make herself a bed, but the dark is coming on too quickly and she returns to the car with just two small branches.

For the umpteenth time she counts the matches still in the book — eight — and decides she can sacrifice another one or two. She pulls some twigs out from under the car where she'd put them to keep dry, stuffs them beneath the branches, lights a match, and then starts the whole aborted operation over again, blowing, bending her body over the dead fire, pushing the twigs toward the middle, blowing, blowing, and finally a flame strong enough to fight the snow flickers up. Heather Thorne lets a squeal of joy escape her mouth, immediately regretting her exclamation as it reverberates through the forest, and then she moves closer to the burgeoning fire with frozen hands.

An unfranked envelope addressed to A. A. M. was left in my mailbox during the night. I found it when I was trying to fix the letterbox lever, which had lost one of its screws. I opened it hurriedly, amid the wind and blowing snow, and the envelope fell to my feet. It contained a white sheet, letter size, on which a few words had been written with a black marker: "You're barking up the wrong tree. Heather never had a chance of getting out of there. You should be the first to know that, given that the crime was signed with your initials. A piece of friendly advice: shut your fucking mouth or get out of here before it's too late and it all starts up again."

I read the message a second time and remained at the mailbox, arms dangling at my sides, until the ink started to run in the snow and the letters started to look deformed, "your" becoming "her" — "her initials" — and the word "crime" enlarging and covering the entire page. What crime was I being accused of, I wondered, as black water soaked into my woollen gloves.

I picked up the envelope, now just a wet rag, put it in one of my pockets, went back into the house, and placed it, along with the letter, under a pile of dictionaries so that they'd dry and get their shape back, but the ink permeated the cover of my *Petit Robert* dictionary, imprinting symbols like hieroglyphs on its white exterior.

The letter is now illegible and I am the only person, apart from whoever wrote it, to know its contents, which as the ink dilutes them are gradually becoming more distorted and making me doubt the accusation of the letter and the threat easily read between its lines. How to judge the truth of a message that has been erased? How can you even claim that it was written?

"Particles derive their mass not from themselves but through mating furiously with the void," writes Étienne Klein in *Le monde selon Étienne Klein*, which pushes me to wonder if the writer's weight is the consequence of his own coitus with the void. I rummage furiously in the void, dig it out, and at last open John Gribbin's *In Search of Schrodinger's Cat* in which I have underlined the following phrase in red ink: "An important aspect of the uncertainty principle . . . is that it does *not* work in the same sense forward and backward in time."

I appropriate the sentence and write a few more words on scrap paper: "A text behaves in different ways, depending on whether it draws from the past or anticipates the future. Time varies according to a text being projected forward or backward and the speed at which the past evolves. It is possible to modify the past with a single stroke of a pencil, a single roll of the dice, or by pressing the Delete button. But the trace of the suppressed past lives on."

Then I rip up the scrap paper and ask Holy Crappy Owl if two plus two still makes four. "Five!" he exclaims while he counts the wing feathers he spreads out in front of himself: "Five!"

I don't want to think about Heather. Not now.

———

Sitting near the fire in which only a few embers remain, Heather wonders where she'll go now that the cold and snow have arrived, and then she hears a feeble barking, more like a whine. "Jackson?" she calls out hesitantly. "Jackson, my love?" When another whine reaches her, she jumps up and runs in the direction the moans seem to be coming from.

The anonymous letter is lying on the table in front of P., who is trying in vain to figure it out, since the paper on which it was written is now nothing more than a surface impregnated with washed ink. He also examines my dictionary's dustjacket, on which a few words whose meaning escapes us are imprinted. I pull the paper toward me and repeat from memory the letter's contents, uncertain which possessive adjective preceded "initials" — was it "your" initials or "her" initials — and then draw his attention to the tone of the message, which, despite offering "friendly advice" actually expresses a deep hostility.

P. doesn't like its tone either, nor the anonymity that accentuates the threat. He asks what I've got myself into now, what corpse I've unearthed, to incite such fear, such hatred, and the violence that will necessarily follow. I reply that had I known I was exhuming a dead person's remains when I called Heather Thorne by the only name belonging to her, then I'd probably have hurled the shovel as far away as I could. But it's too late for any of that, the ground has been disturbed and the dead woman unearthed by her creator — if that's not too eclectic a way of explaining Heather Thorne's return from heaven or hell.

I twirl my glass of wine around in my hand, tilt it a little to appreciate its colour, and ask P. what he would do in my position. It's a ridiculous question, he says, because he's not me and I'm not even sure myself what position I've been assigned. So for now, I decide to do what A. A. M. would do: continue writing the novel, continue digging up the earth, until my hand touches the contours of Heather Waverley Thorne's coffin.

Despite her fatigue, Heather is still pursuing Jackson's yapping, but the further she runs, the further away it sounds, as if Jackson were toying with her and wanted to take her back to a different time in her life. She is experiencing the strange sensation of each step being a step in the direction of something forgotten, that she's not moving toward what she could call her future, but sinking into a torpid cycle whose slowness is tied up to the very limits of its own duration. She feels, furthermore, as if she'll soon reach the ultimate boundary, one where time will stop before embarking on its race to a denouement occurring in a forest that is also retreating, folding up on itself in the imperceptible but constant movement of a slight breeze, one that nevertheless makes trees turn and twist in their trunks, millimetre by millimetre, toward the sun in the east, and new beginnings.

Exhausted by the toll of long hours of walking in which all she can rely on to move forward is the gentle wind, she decides to stop for the night, convinced she'll be able to catch up with time's languor and that Jackson will again be there tomorrow to guide her to her final destination.

I lean over the dashboard, which endlessly shows quarter after midnight, and in vain I search for Heather. Close to the Buick, sooty branches resting on a pile of ashes indicate to me that she left some time ago. On the ground, footsteps whose prints have widened come and go in multiple directions and are then lost where the snow has melted beneath the cover of the trees.

I walk around the car and notice that Heather has taken her gun with her. The axe is still lying near the dead fire, though, shining in the light of the third-quarter moon. I grab it and, as I raise my arms and brandish its sharp edge in front of me, I hear a yapping, quickly followed by a wail, and I understand that Heather is about to find Jackson.

December 5. Time is short. I trash Heather's car with the axe. I shatter the front windshield, the rear windshield, tear up the seats, smash in the doors, sweating like a convict and emitting a raucous cry with every blow because I don't want Heather coming back to shelter here. The Buick belongs to another part of the story and I need to move backward if the story is to continue.

This is the only choice I have, and for it to happen I need to gather my notes and my wits and think, think, does A plus B equal C, must focus on Heather and Jackson, must pay one last visit to Vince, to Howard W. Thorne, to

Gilles Ferland and Herb McMillan, who lives I don't know where and who might well hold the key to the whole story.

I need, as I said, to think, A times B, to foresee the inevitable obstacles and the possible return of the small woman or maybe one of her acolytes. I must also be on my guard with the author of the letter, someone who might spring into action at any moment, and I need to give P. instructions in case things go wrong, how to repair the fences, clear the paths, what do I know? I must act quickly if I want to relive Heather Waverley Thorne's death before she does.

Things aren't right. Things aren't right at all. The storm that washed us out a few days ago is merely a memory now, and the mild early-December temperature is hindering Heather's walk toward her past and thwarting my plans. I need another storm, I need uncontrollable winds that will blind the clouds and hold us hostage to the story coming our way.

Not knowing to whom I should turn, I call the cats into my study for a summit conference with Holy Crappy Owl, but the cats, what with their logic too simplistic to follow my ratiocinations, don't understand my story at all. As soon as I start talking about Jackson's yelping they start yawning, their way of telling me dogs hold no interest for them and advising me to get some sleep.

But the cats don't know that sleep no longer soothes me, that my nights are no more than a series of equations with interchangeable variables: H. W. equals A. A.; A. A.

plus A. A. equals P.; when you subtract A. and A. from H. W. you get Bev; P. is bigger than R., but is R. the same as V.? How are the cats to know my dreams are filled with strangers who take turns hiding behind the features of a little woman who squeals her car tires along roads where evanescent deer and dogs are resting?

Only Crappy gets excited as my story progresses, imploring me to find the small woman again, to lock Ferland and McMillan up before the next storm, to hide Heather in the attic and get a gun like hers. "You can find one," he shouts, "you can find one, now hurry." He is even more horrified than I am by the illegible letter and convinced it won't stop there, that after the letter will come stones thrown through the windows, dead rats on the doorstep, slashed tires, who knows what, *hurry!*

I order him to be quiet for a minute: "Shut up, Crappy." His cries are making my head spin, and his jumping around and making his string swing from left to right, his twisting it around himself and attempts at a few pirouettes mean I have to get up and untangle the cord from his neck. "Crappy, shut your fucking mouth! Please!" But Crappy doesn't get what I'm saying and carries on jiggling around shouting, "Gun, Andrée, gun, bang!"

Réal Morissette is staring at his brother, Vince, as he stands hunched over the photo that he's been unable to put out of his mind ever since that so-called Beverley, may the devil take her, talked to him about Heather and Jackson. He slides it into one of his coat pockets when he goes out, places it on the table during mealtimes, even takes it to bed with him, and Réal is convinced both of them will end up crazy if Vince doesn't let go of the damn photo. He extends an arm to grab it but Vince, his face a thundercloud, slams his palm down on the photo and then goes up to his bedroom without a word.

He lies down fully dressed on the bed, the photo beside him, and thinks back to that November day when Réal, Heather, Jackson, and he had gone for a picnic in La Languette despite the chilly weather because nothing made them happier than warming their fingers around a thermos of steaming coffee and watching the river flow by.

Vince has forgotten why Réal had accompanied them. Because he was his brother, simple as that. Because he liked the river, black coffee, and Heather's company. Maybe too much, he thinks, and suddenly the urge to scream overwhelms him, rips his chest open, because he is wondering now if Réal, his brother—his only real friend, his confidant, dammit—has something to do with Heather Waverley's death, and if all his solicitude actually originates in a guilt predating the photograph, which would be based on his coveting the forbidden object and his desire to possess it at any cost.

He extends an arm to light the lamp on his nightstand and looks at the photo again, a photo taken by a young man in love, Beverley had concluded. But Vince Morissette, diminished by his sleepless nights, sees nothing in it but the work of a traitor.

Heather Thorne is lost in the heart of a forest darkened by the constant December clouds and no longer knows where she is. This morning, her first thought when she woke up was for Jackson. "Jackson!" she cried out hoarsely, and the dog answered her. To get to him, she needed to follow the line formed by the three birches facing her, and then take the path chainsaws had clear-cut behind them. But before that, she needed water, more water, because the lining of her throat was so dry that tears sprang to her eyes every time she tried to swallow. She had to find a stream or a spring, clear water on a bed of stones.

She found one by taking a left beyond the birches and making her way to a clearing where she turned forty-five degrees to the right after skirting around a huge glacial boulder covered in moss. She scratched an arrow in it with her fingers to show her the way to go on her return. Bent over the stream, she thanked an invisible heaven for having led her there, and looked for a hollow object she could use to store water for the thirsty hours ahead. She tried to shape a piece of bark to use as a container, but the effort was futile. Never mind, under this magnanimous heaven other streams would flow.

Before she left, she checked how the wound on her right thigh was doing. She noticed it had reopened, which didn't surprise her as time seemed to be moving slowly backward. Using the previous landmark to guide her, she retraced her steps as far as the mossy boulder, but it had disappeared, and the clearing and birches too. As for Jackson's yelping, now it seemed to be coming from everywhere at the same time, as if she were stuck in a bowl or cavity, inside which echo answered echo.

Heather Thorne was on her own, alone with four Jacksons calling out to her for help, lost in the interlacing of a maze opening onto a past that only she could solve.

Heather has disappeared. I send this affirmation out like an arrow that crashes into the wall, just missing its target and making the lamp wobble, its light casting waves over P., who notices neither the arrow nor the lamp illuminating first his left and then his right eye as it rocks back and forth. I hesitate to tell him the news, convinced he's going to tell me that it's impossible for a character to escape like that, but he reflects for a moment, the lamp now lighting up his whole face, and asks me how I plan to find her.

Is he serious or just playing along with me? Seeing that he's waiting for an answer, I admit that I've not really thought out a plan yet: Heather's departure has put me in an unpredictable situation which will lead me to an impasse. It seems sensible to wait for the snow and the coming storm to search for Heather, just like Vince and

Howard W. Thorne did earlier—but with the advantage, this time, of having a head start.

"Dangerous," says P., and Crappy, listening at the doors, repeats the word. "Dangerous, Andrée, dangerous, *gun, bang!*" I pay no heed to Crappy's warnings, because the texture of the silence enveloping our words has changed, all of a sudden. I glance outside and notice that the rain, which had stopped at dawn, has started again and is hammering the roof with its heavy pattering.

Herb McMillan's house, built on the edge of a river feeding into Two Hill Lake, looks, from a distance, like an abandoned cabin. But I'm not fooled, because fresh tire tracks lead to the house. The closer I get, though, the straighter the walls stand, ultimately revealing a solid wooden house with no ornament other than a rack of moose antlers above the door. A man's house. A hunter's house.

Following the footprints on the muddy path, I creep around the house and hold my hands up like a visor to the window of the back door and make sure McMillan isn't home. I push the door open, and it swings back with a sinister grinding noise that gives me pause. I call out to McMillan, in case he's in the back room, and take my boots off on a braided rug where another pair as dirty as mine has been placed. Out of caution, I call again, and then start inspecting the house.

I'm not sure what I'm looking for, but I know I'll find something, what with McMillan being the only one who's not revealed anything yet. I open one of the kitchen cupboards, rummage in drawers, and tiptoe to the back, to what must be the bedroom. I grip the door handle, try to turn it, but it's locked. What I'm looking for is in this room, this closed room I'm already thinking of as an ogre's lair. Eventually I find the key at the bottom of a jar and, heart thumping, insert it into the lock, afraid that McMillan is hiding behind the door ready to jump me as soon as the inevitable squeak is heard. With my foot, I push it open anyway, and, expecting McMillan to appear, retreat in the same motion, but the bedroom is empty. In the darkness I can see the luminous halo emanating from a thin metal object — my computer — which I take to the kitchen table.

In the pale light of the screen, I click on the file named *Back Roads*, and find in it all the corrections and additions I've made since the computer was stolen, all of them, including the pages of the last few weeks and the ones I've not yet written, but which are, I know, identical to the ones I shall write. The novel is already there, complete, and can no longer be changed.

It's raining when I race out of McMillan's house. My unlaced boots stick in the soft ground and I can see the rain streaming into the river, agitated by swirls. It's written: "agitated by swirls." An apocalyptic light, because the end is near, pierces the foggy summits of the two hills, and I collapse right when I'm about to grab my door handle. It's written.

It's written.

The rain snakes around my neck, wets my already matted hair, and jumps into the puddle that will reach my mouth in a moment or two. The heavy noise of the falling rain surrounds me, mingling with the pattering on the car and the rushing of the river toward the lake.

The light dims and, little by little, the puddle of water grows until it reaches my mouth, which fills with the taste of mud and metal. I lean up on my elbows, even though it feels really good to be lying there at one with the rain-swollen earth, grab the car door handle at last and get into the car. Once I've shed my coat I turn the heating up to full blast. Ahead of me, Herb McMillan's house is collapsing into the river, detritus floating away with the current. Herb McMillan doesn't exist. Herb McMillan is nothing more than one of the other names I've given myself.

I've put on some dry clothes but I'm still shivering. A cup of tea steams in front of me, and I pick it up with two hands and hold it to my cheek, my chest, and then to the inside of my wrist, from which the heat travels to the rest of my body.

On the television, Kevin Bacon is playing Ryan Hardy in *The Following* and points his gun at a serial killer, or maybe it's his own reflection in the mirror, I've lost the thread of the story, because the noise of the shot and broken glass resonates as far as the forest where Heather, at the sound of the explosion, throws herself on the ground, near a hollow where rain has formed a pond and the water fills her mouth with a taste of bark and lichen.

The unreadable letter, which now has the texture of an old piece of parchment on the verge of crumbling, is on my black table between a growing pile of books and the cream-coloured poinsettia that is my only concession to Christmas decorations this year. Holy Crappy Owl protests, because he misses the company of the twin owls who wave their wings over the table at the solstice; Holy and Crappy, whom he thinks of as nephews resident in some faraway country and visiting just to join him in the singing of "It's the Most Wonderful Time of the Year." I tell him Holy and Crappy are waiting for the snow — like Heather, like me, like everyone — and that they can't travel here until the storm carries them. "Even Santa Claus is waiting for the snow, for fuck's sake!" I yell, and the cat wakes up, glares at me with slanted eyes, and then jumps out of his armchair and goes upstairs.

It's December 10 today, so Heather must have been dead for three days, but time is stagnating and stretching out, extending the balminess of October into the darkness of Advent and its crazy rabbit-stew mix of rain, snow, slush, and sludgy mud, the deerskin mittens I bought to protect myself from the La Languette cold of no use to me now. Reluctantly, I turn back to reconstituting the events surrounding Heather's death.

In other circumstances, the mild weather would fill me with joy, but I have a murder to solve, or perhaps a murder to commit in order to solve it, depending on how you see it, because the only important thing is solving the mystery of Heather Waverley Thorne's disappearance and reappearance.

And there's the letter on the black table which never leaves my peripheral vision, the letter totally contradicting the revelation that made me fall back into my chair in Herb McMillan's house — because if the story I'm so keen to reconstruct is already written, how would shutting my mouth change anything about it?

There are too many people populating the story, too many hands trying to rewrite Heather Waverley's already written past. I need to take back control of the situation and, as soon as the first storm appears, rush into the desolate woods of La Languette. And if the storm doesn't come by itself, I'll have no other choice but to induce it, the way you induce a birth, and to try to interpret Heather Thorne's last cries though the furious whistling of the wind.

The languorous notes of Erroll Garner's "Misty" fill the house, interrupted only by the light clicking of my fingers as I type, "The languorous notes of Erroll Garner's 'Misty' fill the house."

My face is no longer becoming paler, probably because time is stagnating. Nonetheless, I powder my cheeks a little, and Vince's too. He's been breathing a little easier what with the rain averting the coming snow but he's still worried, because he knows the snow will inevitably arrive. He takes advantage of the reprieve to put chains on his truck's tires, fix the brakes, change the oil. He wants to be ready when Howard W. Thorne knocks at his door to drag him off in search of Heather. I point out that snow chains are banned now, to which he replies that no ban is going to stop him from saving Heather this time and that, if we follow the logic of the events we're preparing to live through, they'll be taking place in 1980.

The powder I'd applied to my cheeks disappears instantly. Vince is right: I didn't need to induce the storm, because it had already taken place—because it started on December 7, 1980. All we need to do is wait for the disturbance of time to carry us there. I hold out the Vise-Grip that Vince, lying under his truck, has asked for. Its handles are stained with black oil residue that I wipe on my cheeks.

The bitterness of the water on her cracked lips carries Heather far away from the forest, onto a beach covered in brown seaweed that the rising tide washes over her face and then carries back out to sea with each shushing of the waves. Her body half submerged, Heather wants to be as supple as the seaweed and float with it. She smooths her hair, stretches out her arms, and hears the faint strains of a gull calling. Jackson, she thinks. Jackson, she wants to shout, but the powerful tide enters her dry throat. Jackson, she thinks again as morphing red and black shapes cover the milky sky. Thrusting her hips, Heather eventually manages to arch her body back and spit out the pure water obscured by the seaweed. "Jackson . . ." But the cries drowning in her parched throat turn into groans, hoarse gargling sounds in the forest's icy air.

As she sits in the pond tasting of bark and lichen, all of Heather's limbs are trembling. I'm going to die here, she thinks, I'm going to die in this endlessly identical forest before I've even confronted the men driven mad by their culpable desires. Then a scream from beyond the trees shakes her, an interminable whine that rips through all parts of the forest..Gathering up every last bit of strength, Heather Waverley Thorne supports herself on her hands, unfolds her stiff legs, and walks unsteadily in the direction of a phantom dog's destiny.

I wipe the mirror with the palm of my hand and bring my face closer to the reflected being in the misty surface attempting to identify me; I stare hard at the worried expression my breath is fogging up again, and in a low voice say, "My name is Heather, Heather Thorne," at the same time as my distressed reflection.

"Heather Waverley Thorne is my doppelgänger," I finally say to the person looking at me — to my double — and then I start to laugh, aware that after taking cover behind a legion of doubles, today I find myself standing in front of my exact and ghostly counterpart, come from I don't know what fantastical universe, from I don't know what parallel world destined to meet my own, so that here before the mirror I should ask which one, out of my reflection and me, actually possesses some reality. And I laugh and I laugh, while the mirages crumble away.

My past has taken on a dimension that surpasses what remains of my future, and I turn toward it, toward a long and dusty road where my steps sink into the shadow of trees, when the day's brightness, some mornings, awakens no joy in me, no emotion, no hope. I sit down in my black leather armchair, let the sun warm my face, and summon the memory of clear mornings of earlier times, of the walks I took with Miro, my Uncle Lorenzo's dog, just as dawn was breaking. And I walk, with Miro at my side, on the gravel path of the 4th Line, happy simply to be alive and enjoying the privilege of a solitude reinforced by the melancholy of the mist-covered fields.

Sometimes, when my head isn't heavy with weariness and fitful sleep, all I have to do is close my eyes and once more I can feel the fullness of August afternoons smelling of wild apple trees and ripe hay, once more I can make sand pies that I line up on the dock. I am eight years old and know nothing of death. I'm fifteen years old and running with Miro, wanting to seize what is most beautiful from the world, unaware that it is precisely this beauty that I'll draw on when I grow too tired to put on my boots and coat and I plunge my hands in the cold sand.

I'm fifteen and I don't yet know, when Miro runs over and presses his head to my thighs, that from the far side of the first curve hiding the horizon, a Buick will soon appear, and I'll recognize myself at the steering wheel, looking for Miro in the ditch, looking for Miro in the undergrowth, desperately calling out, "Jackson, Jackson, my love."

Jackson is the name of all the dead dogs, dead cats, dead fathers, friends, and loved ones. Jackson is the name of my necropolis. Jackson, my love.

I read somewhere that if a person meets their doppelgänger they'll die within three days. Will the story that I'm telling, then, be over in a few hours — like in one of those dreams where time contracts? Have I really lived through two winters since I first wrote, "I must be called Heather," or did I merely imagine I'd lived them in order to keep the moment of death at bay, the moment of writing "I must be called Heather, she must be called Heather"?

An intense cold has followed the rain. The fields are frozen, and the paths covered in a layer of rough ice that hurts the cats' feet, as well as the wild turkeys', the hares', the rats'. The trees emit eerie creaks and the landscape feels as though it might rip in two, that a thin streak will cleave the sky and run straight to the ground, where it will spread out like a fault line and split open the earth as the forest collapses in thousands of shards of glass that land in the hardened snow.

As I sit inside the car, the condensation of my breath settles on the windows, where a thin frost is forming. I am scarcely able to hold my pen, which squeaks over the lined paper on which I'm writing "river, cross, thistle, lichen, ray" in the hope of remembering, when I go home, the layout of this place and of the river in particular, its waters emerging here and there between ice banks, beneath which you can see, if you stand on the bridge, other layers of ice gnawed at and pitted by the current. The movement of the water is incessant as it changes direction over the rocks, branches, and innumerable obstacles piled up on the riverbed.

With numb fingers, I put the cap back on my pen, pull on my deerskin mittens and open the door. I run to the river, lean over the side of the bridge, and engrave a few words etched on my brain: lace, relief, crystal, false turkey tail, *Trametes versicolor*, and on my way back I stop in front of the iron cross decorated with a hollow metal heart where there used to be a bleeding heart surrounded with thorny branches.

Once I'm back in the car, my glasses fog up again. In order to note what I saw, I must turn on the engine and run the heating. "Cross, heart, thistles, broken swells of the river under which layers of ice on top of each other look like black rays, uneven hilly areas, big semicircular mushrooms, false turkey tail, *Trametes versicolor*, like the ones you see on dead trees in any season," I write, and then I turn the heating off.

In the too-perfect silence that accentuates the noise of each of my movements—the rustling of my coat, the rubbing of my thigh against the seat—I wipe the melting frost off the front window and observe the rusting wayside cross amid the dried thistles and alders. I'm amazed that no monument to Heather, however simple, has been erected near the stone pedestal on which the cross is mounted, and write in my notebook, "No cross for Heather," then draw a crucifix in the frost forming once more on the windshield, through which I can see a white ribbon tied to a road sign on the other side of the bridge, flapping in the wind. I decide the ribbon is for Heather, and that someone, Vince or Howard W. Thorne, replaces it when it gets dirty or frayed, just as people replace withered flowers on graves.

I turn the engine back on and wait until I can see clearly before taking to the road. I'm just about to leave when a grey truck slows down when it's level with my vehicle and the driver leans over to look at me. This is the second driver that has passed since I parked near the bridge, the second driver who's given me a mistrustful look, no doubt convinced that a woman alone in her vehicle at the crossroads of La Languette and the Saint-Joseph Line is up to no good. I smile to indicate everything is fine, but he doesn't reciprocate. He'll be among those who accuse me, a woman on her own on a freezing day, when Heather disappears and we find her lifeless near a sleeping tree. Whatever. At the risk of freezing her fingers, at the risk of seeming crazy, at the risk of being accused of crimes that she didn't invent, an author must return to the scenes of her drama.

———

I should have thrown myself into the river. I've been obsessing over this idea since it got dark, seeing the slow water again, my body leaning over the edge, the black line waving on the stony bottom, and I feel again the slight vertigo that made me forget the cold, as the river, stifled beneath the ice, murmured, *Come, come.*

Heather has also heard the words, *Come, come*, whispered by what could only have been death, but resists with all her strength, because, if Jackson is still on the run, it cannot be her time yet.

She cocks her ear, tries to figure out where the voice attempting to seduce her originates. She realizes that it is very close by: behind her back, near her neck, caressed by an icy breath, on the ground over which a wind is blowing that wants to drag her onto paths that are folding up and closing to push her toward the centre of a labyrinth where the whisperings will devour her.

No! She will not give in. She turns around sharply and forges on, exhaling hot breath as she flees, and the voice diminishes, caught in the sweeping embrace of a golden larch in the middle of its last rustlings.

According to P., Freud's concept of the *unheimlich*, the uncanny, should be translated as "intimate strangeness" and not "worrying strangeness," because the worrying aspect of the strangeness in question is entirely the product of its familiarity, of what comes from the depths of our being and we call "intimate."

The anxiety I feel in front of a mirror has to do with

the familiarity of the reflection I am looking at, with the disconcerting resemblance between the image thrown back at me and the idea I have of a face — my own — that I've never seen except in photos people say are of me, or in mirrors reflecting my mimicry.

I drive on the highway with P., who put a CD in the car's player at the junction of the 610 and the 10, which we renamed Jake Bugg's Highway, what with our having listened to Bugg's first album a dozen times or more as we drove along it under pouring rain or heatwave suns prompting us to turn the AC up to max.

But today, P. has chosen a Steve Earle album, *The Low Highway*. A slight aroma of tobacco is floating in the car, and Earle has just started singing "Remember Me" in his Texan accent. I have to force myself not to cry, because this is the way I'd like to be remembered — "on some sunny day," "on a stormy night," under skies washed clean and brooding winds blow.

I blink away the tears that are blurring the road and say, "That's what I'd like to have written on my gravestone," but P. doesn't hear me. P. is singing the first words of my epitaph, "Remember Me," along with Steve Earle.

Howard W. Thorne is pacing up and down outside his house, stirring up dust, visible in the thin rays of light, that has accumulated over the course of the preceding week. A moment ago, he tried to start reading *The World According to Garp* again, in memory of Heather, because he has nothing more to offer her now but thoughts. But he can't do it. Every time he reopens the book, he breaks off at page 132, unable to proceed—as if the book stops at that page and there is nothing else to be added.

Sometimes, he also has the impression there's nothing else to be added to his life—that he moves around, alone and in limbo, and that no soul awaits its release. Nobody has visited him for a very long time, nobody has come to spy on him from the undergrowth, nobody has skirted around the house while he is out. It's as if his entire existence has suddenly been forgotten, as if he's been abandoned on page 132 of a novel that will never go further than that page.

Tired of going in circles, he pours himself a glass of Wild Turkey, stations himself at the window and waits for some event—a storm, a blizzard, a squealing of tires at the end of the drive—to pull him out of his torpor.

The village cemetery looks like an enormous ice field, out of which, almost perfectly ordered, headstones have shot up, as if someone had cultivated them in order to remind people that whatever is put into the ground always ends up resurfacing.

I am standing in front of my father's grave. It's covered in a thin layer of ice which is fraying in the rain, and I can read, through the thin gaps that separate sections of it, the first letters of the word "Remember." I raise my head and notice the same letters in relief on all the stones in this field of ice. Surely it is the same on the mountain, where a block of pink granite immortalizes Heather Waverley Thorne's name.

I lift my hood up over my wet hair, trace the final letters of "Remember" on my father's tombstone, and tell myself it's time the rain stopped, time Heather returned to the ground, and for the pieces of the jigsaw I've been scattering for the past two years, in my study and on the roads around the village, to finally fall into place.

Tomorrow, Heather will find Jackson and, in so doing, sign her death warrant.

IX.

Heather exits a tiny clearing and finds the arrow she'd scraped into the moss and the three birches she was using to orient herself. She climbs the strongest of the three, which nevertheless bends under her weight, but all she can see ahead of her are branches, branches, and more branches. She calls Jackson's name anyway, and a faint howling reaches her from what, judging from the position of the sun, she thinks is the south. She climbs back down the tree feeling as though her thigh wound is opening up even further, but she runs and runs and runs. Toward the sun.

Toward Jackson.

I've opened a bottle of the Ardèche wine I've been saving in the basement for a special occasion, and clink my glass against P.'s. "To us," I say, smiling at P. in a manner that elicits his own tenderness and the myopic sweetness of his light brown eyes, and then I swallow the Ardèche wine remembering the thousands of moments of tenderness that have accumulated between us, and I smile again, if a little sadly this time, because this meal we are beginning might be our last if the rain turns, as I have predicted, into an endless snow thrashing in the raging wind.

"To us," P. replies, and a sharp gust rattles the house from foundations to attic.

I wait for P. to fall asleep, then I borrow an old backpack of his into which I stuff a change of clothes—wool socks, scarves, mittens, sweaters—slipping among them a flashlight, new batteries, a hunting knife, and wooden matches. Then I clip an axe to the rings on the straps and head to my study to wait for the storm as Vince and Réal Morissette, sitting at Vince's table, listen to the stove clock ding—one ding per minute, every time the second hand reaches the twelve—stringing out endless time made more oppressive by the atmosphere in the room. In front of them are two bottles of beer, two glasses, two plates, and two rare steaks, but neither brother is eating. Occasionally they bring the glasses to their lips, but they don't touch their knives or forks. The wind outside is screaming, and the tension in the dimly lit room is palpable. A kilometre away, standing in front of a window outside which the branches of a Virginia pine are waving, Howard W. Thorne is in the throes of an anguish that doesn't allow him any kind of coherent thought, and he hears the sound of barking approach.

The wind is whistling furiously at the tops of the trees, but here on the spongy ground where the roots snake, its fury barely touches Heather at all. She stops for a moment to catch her breath and sees Jackson appear, a ghostly shadow slipping into the undergrowth. So she shouts again, but the more she shouts the further away the shadow gets. Then a path appears in front of her, which leads to a gravel road. She heads along it, panting like a lame dog, and sees Jackson in the middle of the road, a fuzzy shadow pierced by the flight of a solitary thrush. "Jackson," she murmurs, but a rumbling can be heard beyond the mound on which the animal is standing, the sound of a truck being driven at top speed by two drunk young men, who run it through the vanishing body of Jackson, my love.

The throbbing of the engine as it continues on its way is followed by a wail resonating from the mountain to the village and the 2nd Line.

Holy Crappy Owl stiffens at the end of his string, rigid with horror, "Jackson, boom, boom, dog, blood," he squawks, as a few sheets of paper blow around the room: "Heather on the 4th Line," "Heather and the caterpillars," "Heather drinking at a stream." I gather them up and try to arrange them in some sort of order despite the trembling of my hands. Howard W. Thorne is still standing in the dark and drops his glass. A trickle of amber alcohol runs over the worn rug and soaks into the final pages of *The World According to Garp* while Vince Morissette, his stomach gripped by fear, quickly gets up from the table to run to a black window lashed by the wind.

Heather looks in vain for Jackson's body in the ditches and undergrowth where he might have taken shelter if he was hurt, but there's no longer any sign of the animal, not even a spot of blood on the road. All that remains of Jackson are the infinite tears of the woman kneeling by the road, her hands dirty, her eyes red, and her face so pale you'd think all her blood was draining out from the wound on her right thigh, a long diagonal cut across the limb, staining her pants with a dark spot spreading toward the knee.

Struggling to her feet, she moves a few steps forward and notices a house among the trees. In one of its windows, she can make out a photograph. She draws closer and realizes the picture is of a young girl pointing a gun straight ahead of her. She scrunches her eyes and peers at the young girl, increasingly certain that she knows her. She cups her hands around her eyes and presses her nose against the cold window but the young girl's face blurs as the glass mists over. She takes a step back and wipes the mist with the back of her hand. The contact between the leather and wet glass produces a squeaking sound that makes her shiver, and she looks at the photograph again.

After a few minutes that seem like hours, Heather stumbles, her breath halting. She has just recognized the young girl, whose face she has recently seen in the forest, deformed by the Buick's broken mirror. A single name goes through her mind, one name pushing its way in: *Heather*. She stands there with her arms dangling, repeating this incredible truth: "My name is Heather, Heather Waverley Thorne."

The first snowflakes are beginning to fall. I grab the backpack I've borrowed from P. and, after petting the cats, turn out my study light and leave without looking back. I'm afraid of seeing the cats' silhouettes against the house windows and wanting to retrace my steps at top speed in order to take them in my arms, consigning my manuscript to the garbage and then lying down by P.'s warm side in the ordinary progression of days. But I know that in Herb McMillan's bedroom, my computer is blinking, and the narrative, whether I like it or not, will continue just as it has been written, in the middle of a storm that will block all the roads before dawn.

I lower my head and walk into the wind, brush the car off quickly, throw P.'s backpack inside, and go into reverse without another glance at the house and its inhabitants. The road is already white, and in the headlights the evening is nothing but shimmering sparkles.

Unable to bear his silent house any longer, Howard W. Thorne has jumped in his truck to go look for the barking. Ahead of him, a few snowflakes are mingling with the rain and forming a curtain of crystalline reflections interlaced with the white flakes falling softly from the black sky, reducing visibility and revealing the road only a little at a time — as if it didn't exist until the headlights penetrated each new zone, erasing itself once the vehicle had passed, sinking into a void only other headlights have the power to fill.

In the pitch black surrounding him, Howard W. Thorne is conscious of a new worry surfacing within him and is burdened by a feeling of imminent catastrophe concealed in the darkness enveloping the snow.

Standing in front of the bay window in his living room, Vince Morissette has a sensation exactly like the one that made Howard W. Thorne go out to check the sides of the roads. He turns off the ceiling light, the better to see in the night, and mumbles, "Here we go, it's starting again, an accident's going to happen soon, on the mountain or in the woods." He smooths his hair back in a gesture of powerlessness, and carries on watching the snow being plastered against the window by the wind.

Behind him, his brother is a broad silhouette motionless in the archway leading to the living room. He is hoping the snow will bury the whole of the region and, at the same time, engulf Heather Waverley Thorne's cries in the cottony whiteness of a finally consummated winter.

Heather didn't have any trouble finding the ammunition she was looking for. She slips the bullets for her gun into a canvas bag and goes upstairs to look for warm clothes in the bedroom that used to be hers. Nothing has changed since the last night she spent in the house, she's not sure how many years before, not the thin cotton curtains, not the Virginia Woolf novels, not the teddy bear called Hector William, but she doesn't have time to delay because the storm outside is growing in strength.

Exasperated by his brother's silence, Vince Morissette brusquely turned around: "What do you know about all this?" he asked, but Réal Morissette, faced with an imminent event that has already happened, finds it impossible to tell true from false. In fact, he knows better than anybody, ever since the woman agreeing to be called Beverley showed up in their lives, that the drama which shook the village thirty-five years before is due to happen again and that nobody can predict its outcome nor foresee the consequences. Who can actually determine if the repetition of this event will just be a simulacrum, or if the new drama will gloss over the earlier one, striking from memory the savage winter in which a teenager disappeared?

He lowers his head and says quietly, "I don't know anything anymore, Vince. All I know is that something's going to happen, tonight or tomorrow, and I don't want to be mixed up in it. Good night, brother, and be careful."

Unable to look his brother straight in the eyes, Réal Morissette, with death in his soul, grabs his coat, pulls on his boots, and goes out into the incipient storm. He'd done what he could to keep the woman Vince misguidedly believes to be Beverley, Beverley Simons, a young girl whose eyes are too gentle to provoke mourning, away from the house, but his plans got screwed up and from that point on the rest was beyond his control. He gives Vince a last wave, and his brother makes a movement as if to follow but reconsiders. He needs to be at home when Howard W. Thorne comes knocking on his door to ask for his help.

Through the window where he can see the blizzard starting, Vince watches as his brother's tail lights become smaller in the blowing and increasingly heavy snow. And Réal takes advantage of Vince no longer being able to make out his truck to park on the ever-less-visible shoulder and wipe away the tears blurring his vision. "Heather," he says softly, putting his head in his hands, "Waverley." And then he sees the young girl again, stretched out on a camp bed and white as the death that had insinuated its way into her veins. "*Tabarnak*, Gilles, tell me you didn't do that." And Gilles Ferland started to bawl, yelling and swearing, "Yes, I did it, fuck, I did it, I couldn't see straight, I went crazy, Réal, crazy like I'd lost my fucking head, like it wasn't me in charge anymore."

"We can't leave her like that," was all Réal Morissette had said, cursing the day he'd become friendly with Gilles Ferland. Then he'd washed the young girl, her grazed hands, her body, and her blanched face, saying, "Christ, you're beautiful, Heather," before taking her back into the woods where maybe someone would find her and dig her a proper grave. In truth, Réal Morissette's only crime had been going to see Gilles Ferland in his cabin in the woods on December 11, 1980, finding Heather Waverley Thorne there, a sleeping beauty in the forest, and keeping his mouth shut—his great big fucking mouth—because he knew nothing in the world would ever resuscitate Waverley's unbearably dazzling smile.

As soon as he was back in the house, Howard W. Thorne smelled something new, or rather something old and familiar, a perfume from the past that brought to mind the nearly frozen waters of streams. Immediately, he ran up the stairs to Heather's bedroom and noticed that the red anorak and several other items of clothing had disappeared. He searched the house from top to bottom and realized that the two boxes of bullets he kept as spares had also disappeared, and then his eyes fell upon a photo of Heather and Jackson. A sharp pain ran through his chest for a moment, and he went closer to it.

During his absence, the smile Heather was wearing in the photograph had been wiped away, and the yellow-circled irises of the woman who'd been reading *Paterson* had appeared in the young girl's eyes.

No longer understanding what was happening, Howard W. Thorne bent down to look at the photograph. *You aren't who you think you are.* He grabbed it, smashed it against his knee, and threw it at the dirty wall facing his armchair. His eyes wet with tears, he stepped back, treading on his alcohol-soaked copy of *The World According to Garp*, and rushed out into the storm.

———

The bad weather has redoubled its efforts while I've been out. I can barely see thirty feet in front of me and can already feel the resistance of the snow settling on the road. When I get to the mountain road where I'd hoped to find Heather, I see, through the gusts, an approaching vehicle signalling with its headlights. I slow down, open my window, and wait, snow blowing into the car, for the vehicle to reach me. Its driver also opens his window, and I see the defeated face of Réal Morissette, who barely seems surprised to see me.

"Don't go any further," he shouts through the shrieking wind. "The roads are going to be blocked before long, though I suppose there's no point warning you. *When it's written, it's written*, right? Even if you're barking up the wrong tree, Andrée A., the wrong tree altogether."

Then, without giving me time to reply, Réal Morissette shifts into gear and carries on down into the village. I put on my four-way flashers, which intermittently tint the blowing snow orange, and drive along the verge hoping I'll not be crashed into by a driver hurrying to get home before the storm stops him. Réal Morissette is right—in a couple of hours, none of the roads in the area will be passable, but I don't care much about that right now because Réal has inadvertently revealed that he was the one who sent me the anonymous letter, that he was the person trying from the very beginning of this story to dissuade me from writing it. But it's too late, because other people have written it in my stead.

I brush off the snow covering my knees and thighs, turn the car around, and head for La Languette before

I get stuck on the road halfway there. I'm alone on this road and its diminishing visibility, alone with my ghosts.

Heather is calling herself every name under the sun for not having thought of taking the old snowshoes no doubt still hanging in the shed adjoining the mountain house. She could turn back, but knows that any backward move would mean a return to the limbo she's inhabited for far too long. Luckily, the snow is accumulating less rapidly in the forest that she knows like the back of her hand, having taken the paths along which she's currently struggling dozens of times as a child.

In the thick of night, snow and wind are buffeting the heavy smoke leaving the chimney of Gilles Ferland's cabin deep in the woods, and transforming it into curling grey forms taking on the shapes of tortured creatures, gargoyles and hydra, or gorgons whose manes detach from their skulls and wrap themselves around the branches whipping at the darkness of the forest.

In the cabin, Gilles Ferland and Herb McMillan, an empty bottle of Jack Daniel's at their feet, listen to the wind that is making the walls and roof creak so loudly it's as if it wants to rip them right off. They're both silent, both downcast victims of the worry such a storm and its blows incite in even the most hardened of people.

"Shall we go out for a ride?" asks McMillan, and Gilles Ferland stands up without a word to get his helmet and snowmobile suit.

It's 11 p.m. when Howard W. Thorne knocks at Vince Morissette's door. One miscalculated move has him stuck in the snow, and he needs to borrow Vince's vehicle. "I'll come with you," says Vince, and the two men stride out into the night, lowering their heads to protect them from the biting snow. They're not really sure where they're going and what it is they're looking for, but the sense of urgency they feel is making a mockery of rational thought and telling them to act quickly. All that can be seen of them on the road are the car's headlights, fuzzy beams moving silently forward in the blizzard.

The snow is so dense that I have to keep an eye on the fence posts along the side if I'm not to drive right off the shoulder, which is covered in thicker and thicker drifts that intermittently spread across the road and through which the car penetrates with a dull, soft sound. I don't know what point I've reached nor if I'll be able to travel much further before I get stuck, so I press on the accelerator in an effort to outdistance the snow and cleave its succession of waves like so many rocks struck by the hull of a ship in distress.

At the intersection of what must be the Saint-Joseph Line and La Languette, a shape rises up in front of me. It might be Heather, it might be Jackson, or might even be one of those animals that, in fables, block your path to herald death's arrival. And as the shape unfolds, I seem to see an eagle owl with enormous wings opening its beak and emitting a single hoarse cry as it splits the night with its flight. I brake, the bird's wings sweep the sides of the car, and I plough into a white wall that crumbles with a crunching of supple branches.

As the wall collapses, the man called P. wakes up from his disturbed sleep with a start, convinced that his nightmares prefigure some misfortune soon to befall him. Downstairs, the calico meows and the first cat, standing at a window that looks out over the wooden arch beyond which a thousand seasons unspool, looks out into the night with worried eyes.

The numbers on the phosphorescent dashboard clock show quarter after midnight, or quarter after noon, and there's a bloodstain on the inside of the windshield covered with a thick layer of snow. An inky blackness surrounds me and I don't know who I am, where I am, and why I am here. I feel my forehead, wet with some viscous substance, and turn on the windshield wipers, which struggle to clear the snow piled onto the window. All I can see before me are branches, lit up by two luminous cones shining obliquely through the powdery snow falling toward the ground with such velocity you'd think it was fleeing threats in the sky.

It is quarter after midnight.

I try to exit the car and a yowling sound escapes my chest. More blood on my right thigh displays the cause of my wail, at odds with the silence of the blurry night and paralyzing me for a few moments. Once the echo of the cry has receded into my beating heart, I remove my wool scarf and tie it firmly around my thigh, an action that drags out another cry that this time I suppress by biting my lips.

I have to get out of the car, but the door refuses to open. Then I see a backpack on the back seat and the axe attached to it. I manage to grab hold of the backpack and drag it up and over into the passenger seat, where all of its contents fall out: sweaters, matches, woollen socks, the recently sharpened axe blade shining through the lot of them. I grab hold of it and shut my eyes as the glass smashes and a shard embeds itself into the tender skin of my right wrist.

At the intersection of two paths that the snow will soon cover, Heather Thorne thinks she hears a cry for help through the northeastern wind's screaming. She can't figure out the direction it's coming from, but she's certain it's a woman's cry, an injured woman she needs to locate before the men arrive, their faces drunk with the sky's rage. She cocks an ear, holds her breath, and starts walking into the complicit wind that carried the voice to her.

She has barely taken a few steps when she hears roaring sounds competing with the noise of the storm. Snowmobiles, she thinks, and points her gun straight ahead.

Gilles Ferland and Herb McMillan are driving at full throttle along the deserted road, intoxicated by a storm so powerful that earlier it made them feel as if the walls of Ferland's cabin, besieged by the thundering frozen air, might fly away, that its planks of knotty pine might stretch so much that the space would lie open to the ghosts, soon to materialize, of which they were vaguely aware. They've now put the thundering behind them, and despite the din of the engines, their hollers reverberate in the night like shouts of victory over the power of the elements, over the spectres the wind has swept up, over everything that might restrict the liberty of those who choose to ignore the past's constant haunting.

On a different road, perpendicular to the one the snow-mobilers are on, Vince Morissette and Howard W. Thorne curse as they get out of Morissette's truck, having driven it into the ditch after hitting a snowbank and spinning around. The truck is now listing at a dangerous angle at the top of a slope they'd have quickly descended, tumbling into the river at the bottom as its icy waters rush forward, were it not for Morissette's deft manoeuvring.

The two men examine the vehicle, calculating their chances of getting it out of the ditch. Then, after exchanging glances, they decide to continue on foot, despite how thick the snow is and the effort the expedition will take. His hands already frozen, Morissette grips the left door of the truck and reaches inside to grab his mittens, gun, and the thermoses of cognac-spiked coffee he prepared. The ensuing slam of the door marks the departure of Heather Waverley Thorne's father and lover into the murderous night.

————

I managed to get out of the car, but still don't know where I am or how I got caught up in the storm. In the middle of the raging weather, the accumulated sensations of nothing actually linking me to the forest around me, and of my being nothing but a suffering body with neither past nor future — as if I'd arrived in the world in this heap of metal being swallowed up by the snow, and was destined to remain forever by it — have resulted in this dull panic gripping me.

Unable to contain my anguish any longer, I stamp angrily on the ground and start to scream. I sink, with the axe between my legs, into the white terror lacerating my departed memory, and then I hear an approaching roar, the noise of engines pushed to the max. I get up to shout again and then stop dead, halted by a premonition strangely resembling some nebulous memory. And then, as the roaring gets louder, the memory crystallizes, and I understand what's coming: the roaring I hear is the roaring of snowmobiles driven by drunken men feeling invincible. The first is called Ferland, the second McMillan. As for me, my name is Heather, Heather Thorne.

Coming from the other direction, Heather advances toward the snowmobilers driving in circles in a field, tracing figure eights in the soft snow — symbols of infinity if you look at them horizontally. Then they shout loudly, laugh, howl like coyotes smelling blood. They have been made feverish by the storm and the alcohol and their feelings of invincibility, of being more powerful than the wind, of being freer

282

than God. After they've been at it for a few minutes, one of them raises an arm and points to an opening in the forest, and they drive to it, bisecting the circles, loops, and eights the snow is quickly covering over; reclosing the gates of infinity.

The noise of the snowmobiles is becoming dangerously loud and I decide to walk deeper into the forest, even though this means leaving in my wake a trail of footsteps, the smell of urine, long drag marks from my injured leg, and branches broken with my axe. Entire sections of a past I don't understand rush by me in the storm with crazy urgency and press themselves on me as the engines roar. The images speeding past are clear and disturbing, urging me to flee as far away as possible even as a curious sense of destiny convinces me not to leave the area where the snowmobilers are driving.

I focus on the images in my mind, one of which will not leave me. It's an image of a plucked owl yelling at me, *Gun, Andrée, gun, gun, bang!* and the bird keeps insisting, in its strident voice, *Gun!* It's fluttering around the oppressive space of a purple-walled room invaded by a cloud of bombyx I am trying to push aside by throwing the axe in front of me as if it were a scythe. I swipe at branches, decapitate the bombyx, brown and white in the night, mixing in with the snow, and swing until my axe lands in a tree trunk and the owl's squawkings cease.

Andrée, the bird says, *Andrée* . . . I yank the axe out of the tree in which it is stuck and examine my right wrist, where a wound in the shape of a double A confirms my identity. I put a bit of snow on it and hear the laughter of the first and second men, Ferland and McMillan, who have now cut their engines and seem to be just a few metres away. My face is on fire as I resume my fitful walk and try to go faster. This time I'm heading in the same direction.

Gilles Ferland and Herb McMillan are passing a bottle of gin back and forth and laughing at obscene jokes before pissing in the snow and trying to trace the initials of the girl they've been jerking off over for months now, but the letters are clumsy and there's a B for Beverley in the H for Heather, an A in the unfinished W for Waverley, and an undefined consonant with wobbly strokes in the T for Thorne.

They zip up their flies, admire their work, and then, cupping their hands around their mouths, shout at the top of their voices, "Heather, Heather Waverley, Heather Beverley, my love," this only increasing their laughter and obscene jokes.

Heather hears their voices calling *Heather Waverley, Heather Beverley* coming at her left and right through the blowing snow sweeping across the road and into the deepest crannies of the forest. The wind is confusing me, she thinks, the wind wants to make me mad. Seeking out the source of the echoing voices, she turns back the way she came, then hurries toward the centre—toward the spot where the voices converge and will meet fatally. Behind her, a few drops of blood the snow has not yet covered will indicate to the men tearing through the forest that an injured woman passed this way.

Ferland and McMillan had no trouble following Heather Waverley — Heather Beverley, Heather Heather, they really don't care which. They followed the drops of blood and found Heather in the middle of the path, arms dangling by her side, staring, as if she were hypnotized, at a piece of wood in the form of an angel, a Virgin, and a Virgin turned angel with eyelids weighed down by the snow. McMillan takes Heather in his arms and whispers not-so-sweet nothings in her ear, "Fuck me, you have amazing breasts, fuck me, what a gorgeous mouth, fuck me, you have sexy hips. Fuck me, you smell good." But the woman doesn't respond.

"Jesus, are you frozen where you stand?" says Ferland, who then trips in the rush to have his own turn holding her by the waist. In the same movement, he drags the motionless woman down with him and her head, covered with a red tuque, hits a sharp stone.

Hot blood runs down my cold cheek, and the flakes of snow falling from the immense sky are illuminated, one by one, like thousands of tiny red-bodied flies. "Christmas is coming," I say to myself, "Christmas and its twin owls dancing to the tune of 'Jingle Bells.'" Then a man's voice mutters that I'm pretending to have fainted, that I'm putting it on, for Christ's sake, I'm faking it. The voice comes to me through a veil through which I can hear Jackson my love barking, calling out to me from the autumn forest.

I slip between the trees, a winged woman who no longer knows pain, place myself on a gravel path over which orange caterpillars — *Pyrrharctia isabella*, the Isabella tiger moth — migrate, and then see a little girl playing hopscotch, *One, two — one, two*, a little girl with apple cheeks who could be me, Andrée, Heather, or Beverley, who could be childhood and carefreeness. *One, two, three*, she sings, her sneakers reaching the grey of a sky beneath another grey sky rolling its tousled clouds on the hill. I hold my hand out to the clouds and touch them at the exact moment when two booming gunshots resound in the space filled with the whistling of the storm.

With their bodies bent against the strength of the storm, Vince Morissette and Howard W. Thorne struggle forward, their clothes weighed down with snow, as best they can in the dawn's barely perceptible light. In the time that has passed since they left Vince's vehicle, their bodies have lost their heat and they feel as if they'll never reach the place that a past they thought dead and buried is propelling them toward.

Morissette is employing his gun as a cane in order to walk faster, but the wind keeps pushing him back while Thorne, out of breath, turns his back to the storm. He tries to tell Morissette they're never going to make it just as a gust — carrying a familiar sound — bites at their reddened skin. They lift their heads sharply, and a silence born of their worst fears descends around them. Two sharp cracks shake the forest, immediately followed by two more gunshots.

Clutching his chest with both hands, Howard W. Thorne cocks his ear and begs Vince to hurry. "Go, go on, run, please, I'll catch up in a few minutes." Vince hesitates for a moment, worried Thorne is having a heart attack and that he'll be found half-buried in the snow, mouth frozen in pain from the cardiac arrest that felled him as he was trying to call out Heather Waverley's name one last time. But given Thorne's insistence, the younger man obeys and abandons him on the invisible road. Thorne watches Morissette slowly disappear into the blizzard and, uttering God's name, lets himself fall softly back.

With his body arched to withstand the fierce gusts of wind feeding on the open space around him, Vince Morissette slowly, despairingly, plows on. The storm, like an animal in its death throes, is angrily contorting itself and driving him back, and the snow as high as his knees makes him feel as if he's sinking with every step he takes in the deserted stretch of cold dust trying to swallow him.

After a few more minutes of desperate walking, he finally finds shelter in the undergrowth where the snow is not as dense and the wind's roaring can't bite at him. Clumsily, he attempts to wipe away the snot that has dribbled down to his chin with his cold-stiffened mittens. Then he sets off again toward the source of the sound of the gunshots. Near the track dug out by a stream, he sees traces of footsteps at last, and then marks left by snowmobiles' caterpillar tracks. He gathers his strength and runs in the direction of the footsteps and, as Howard W. Thorne asked, toward the place where the violence of thirty-five years before might finally come to an end.

The two swans take off, I think — as well as the wooden angel-Virgin. Beauboule traverses a patch of fog, and writes his name, "Beauboule," and the rain releases me, a few light drops on my burning lips and forehead.

Vince Morissette is the first to recognize Heather's anorak, its scarlet red plainly visible amid the thousands of trees bending beneath the whiteness. "Heather," he shouts, but the anorak doesn't move. He reaches her and immediately understands the horror that has plunged Heather into her torpor. A few metres ahead of her, two men lie belly down in the snow, near a woman with closed eyes, her head leaning on a rock where she appears to be resting.

Seizing Heather Waverley by the arms, he tries to catch her unfocused gaze and begs the young girl to refute the scene in front of her, of lifeless bodies lying on snow-covered ground spattered with red. "Heather, tell me you didn't just do that?" he says, "Heather, tell me, for fuck's sake!" But Heather did indeed shoot Gilles Ferland, two shots it took, and then Herb McMillan, who hadn't noticed a thing. Two shots each: *Bang! Bang!*

Vince gently takes Heather's gun away from her. She doesn't resist. Then he goes to help the injured woman, Beverley Simons, who is talking deliriously about Virgin birds and, unable to reach her arms up to where the birds actually fly, tracing wings on her stomach. Quickly he removes his coat and sweater and tucks them under Beverley's head, dabbing her temples with one of the sleeves. "Go for help, Wave, fast," he says, and Heather Waverley Thorne disappears into the forest without a word.

Early in the morning a dozen police officers arrived with dogs, followed by several snowmobilers eager to help and wanting to mitigate the events, news of which had spread like a trail of powder through the territory. But nobody needed help any longer, and no amount of goodwill could diminish the drama that had occurred in the middle of the blizzard, its delirium so powerful and remembered so vividly that it would be dubbed "The Deranged of December 1980," as the storm which had transmitted its fury and craziness to anyone and everyone who'd had the audacity to venture out in it. Nothing could alleviate the harmful consequences now: Herb McMillan was dead, Gilles Ferland too, and Beverley Simons's blood had drained out onto the fresh snow where two red swans had unfolded their wings.

On December 8, 1980, from dawn to dusk, La Languette had never before been such a screaming forest, screaming along the paths and trails through which police and snowmobilers had roared their engines shouting *Heather, Heather Waverley*, because a young woman had disappeared, leaving nothing behind her but the crime's weapon, an old hunting gun her father had given her when she'd attained the age at which women need to be able to defend themselves.

As for Howard W. Thorne, the delirium touched him where his heart beat, and he needed to be taken out of the forest on a stretcher along the road to La Languette amid winds fighting for the privilege of ravaging the newborn dawn, embracing in wild dances and stealing the breath of the creatures dressed in wool trying to fight its strength and dominance.

The anarchic weather, which made the darkness of uncertain days tip over into the whiteness of endless nights, lasted until Friday, December 12.

That morning, Heather Waverley Thorne was found in a clearing, leaning against a tree and facing the rising sun. It was Réal Morissette—who until then had refused to be involved in the search or a hunt, depending on whether you thought of looking for Heather Waverley Thorne as an attempt to save the life of a woman numbering among the Delirious, or as a criminal investigation—who made the macabre discovery, which could just about be called that if you agreed that the peaceful smile fixed to the young woman's white face could be defined as a vision of horror.

Refusing to touch the body, he'd called for help and sat there, next to Heather, until the engine noise reached him and, on the other side of the clearing, three machines appeared, their bodies reflecting the first rays of sun—like insects whose shining forewings buzz in the luminous dawn.

On the 2nd Line, during those few days in which the region's inhabitants lost any sensible consciousness of the world, the man called P. paced around the rooms of his house, imprisoned by the blizzard that blocked the roads and cut the power, isolating him even more. In a moment of pained rage, he hurled the silent phone against a wall, making a photo of the woman he lived with, Andrée, fall off it. Andrée who had furtively sneaked off into the endless night so she could determine, when the darkness finally disappeared, whether her body would make a shadow on the ground or if she was no more than another woman's shadow.

It seems as though I've been walking for months and months on the unstable terrain into which I sink with each step, and where all my landmarks are melting into a powdery snow that blinds me. I lost the backpack I'd brought with me, I lost Heather, and until this morning, I'd lost my bearings, convinced that the house whose roof I was hoping to eventually see through trees beaten down by the storm had disappeared, just like Howard W. Thorne's house had disappeared. In vain I searched the mountain for his house, but all I found was a structure on the verge of collapse, near which, on a pink granite rock, the initials of a young girl named Heather Waverley, little more than a child, were fading. But at last the light of the sun penetrated the frosty December air and there was the house, intact among the trees, on the hill beyond the arch where the April heat is melting the last few patches of snow.

I watch my body's shadow cut the ground in front of me, its furrows trying to become rivers, and walk through the arch. A man and two cats are watching me from the windows; at first, they don't recognize me, and then they rush to the front door.

Vince has prepared salads, sandwiches, and appetizers and laid them out on the glass table in the middle of the patio. I can see him talking to a woman I don't know in the kitchen where a few guests are gathered, and after he's done he comes out to give me a bottle of cold beer that I clink against his, toasting friendship and life and then drinking in silence, happy that winter is behind us at last. Around the house, the grass is beginning to grow. Two robins alight on the turf but are immediately chased away by Vince's border collie. "Jackson," Vince calls, and the dog bounds up onto the deck and rubs against our legs.

"Do you remember Beverley Simons?" Vince asks suddenly, biting his lip as if memories of the young girl had filled him with nostalgia. "I dreamed about her last night," he says, "a wild and crazy dream set in the woods near the La Languette wayside cross." I answer yes, that I remember Beverley Simons as well as if I'd last seen her yesterday.

We finish our beers and Vince gets up to fetch some wine. "Don't worry," I say, "Leave it to me." The house smells pleasant and spring-like and I stop in the middle of the kitchen to take in the surroundings, which are just as I imagined they would be. Sitting on a small set of drawers is a photo of Vince, taken at La Languette in the company of a young woman who looks strangely like me. "Her name was Heather," says Réal, who's come to join us. "Heather Waverley. She died in a car accident about a week after that photo was taken." I say, "Yes, Heather Waverley, like on the pink granite plaque."

A little later, a few of Réal's friends arrive, two men whose faces are very familiar to me and a small woman whose wide-set toes are exposed in sandals that aren't right for the season. They frown at me, as if I were also familiar to them, though from some more distant, hazy time in their lives. I welcome the diminutive woman with a discreet nod, but she slips away immediately, and I leave the kitchen while the two men, who've taken Réal aside, ask who I am. I can't hear the name Réal gives them, and I prefer it that way.

It's midnight by the time I tell Vince I must be getting back. In my rear-view mirror, I watch his silhouetted figure shrink in the porch light, and I'm not sure if I'll ever see him again.

P. and I take advantage of the vegetation not having grown over the fences yet to put them back up. We work until the middle of the afternoon, our bodies sweating because of the clothes we have to wear so as not to get scratched by the rose bushes. When we're finished, I take a shower and announce to P. that I'm going for a walk on the 4th Line and will be back in time for dinner.

I park the car just before the first bend and follow the lane to the cabin that goes around the hill, barely a hill, where blueberries abound in August. A hundred metres from the road, I enter the forest and walk to a clearing planted with young trees. Through the undergrowth I can make out the carcass of a rusty Buick, the doors of which have been torn off. I move closer, push aside the dry grass, rocks, thistles, and dead leaves that surround and conceal it, and finally find the axe, extremely well preserved, its shining blade reflecting the sun coming through the red trees.

Before retracing my steps, I examine the vehicle's dashboard. The clock has stopped at quarter after midnight. I compare the time on my watch to the clock's and realize that the wound on my wrist has opened up again. I must have aggravated it looking for the axe or caught myself on the rose bushes. I walk back to the road and down to the stream that forks near the ditch and apply a bit of mud to the wound.

An animal—a hare, fox, or porcupine—is sneaking around in the undergrowth behind me when a Buick appears at the top of the hill, its chrome gleaming in the twilight. As the vehicle approaches the animal flees, a few leaves rustle, and a bird takes to the air. When the Buick's driver notices me, she raises her hand in greeting, returns my smile and brushes an impudent lock of hair away from her face. Then her smile freezes, her eyes widen in disbelief, and the lock falls back down onto her forehead as the car skids onto the gravel where the *Pyrrharctia isabella* are laboriously moving forward. A cloud of dust surrounds me as the Buick crashes into the glowing forest in a squeal of blue metal.

When I leave the 4th Line, I know who I am.

My name is Heather Thorne.

Saint-Sébastien-de-Frontenac, March 2014–January 2017

ACKNOWLEDGEMENTS

First of all, my warmest thanks to P., for P. M., with whom I wandered my back roads with a glass of wine. A particular thank you to Y., an old friend who, unbeknownst to him, was my inspiration for the character of Vince.

I would also like to express my sincerest gratitude to the whole Éditions Québec Amérique team for their support and patience. A big thank you to Jacques Fortin, Caroline Fortin, Marie-Noëlle Gagnon, Mylaine Lemire, Nathalie Caron, and everyone else who worked behind the scenes to produce this novel.

Thanks also to the members of the Arachnide team for their own impeccable work. In particular, I would like to thank Noah Richler, who provided me such a warm welcome to the press. Many thanks, also, to Gemma Wain, Maria Golikova, and Joshua Greenspon. Deepest gratitude, at last, to J. C. Sutcliffe, for translating this novel without getting lost in any one of the paths less travelled I explore in it.

And finally, thanks to the Canada Council for the Arts for its financial support.

TRANSLATOR'S NOTE AND ACKNOWLEDGEMENTS

With every translation there is a challenge. For me, for this book, it was most of all the fact that Andrée Michaud's style and voice are very different from how I write, leading to a first draft that was akin to the book writing a straitjacket on. Michaud is an exceptional stylist, and it is a daunting if not impossible task to trace all the tiny whorls and loops of the author's prose. A good translation will land very close to its original, knowing where to swerve away to preserve the text's intention, and when to mimic the French more strictly to convey something crucial. Some translators — including me, usually — often prefer to keep full stops as they are in the original and then punctuate sentences internally as needed, to suit the target language. But this technique could not work for Andrée Michaud's style, given its unusual grammatical constructions, and resulted in ungainly English sentences confusing to parse, let alone to read in any fluent way. Adhering too closely to the original, both syntactically and stylistically, meant, paradoxically, that the text lost some of its character and verve. Thankfully, Noah Richler was a wise and thoughtful counsellor. He persuaded me that I might confidently step further away from the dictates of the French language while still being true to Andrée Michaud's intentions in order to retain the novel's singular voice.

A further note: all quotations of books are from published versions of either the original English or original English translation, except for the quotations from Jean Sioui on page 70 and Étienne Klein on page 241, neither of which have been translated yet. I have done my best to render these with the sensitivity they are due.

I would like to thank Andrée A. Michaud, Noah Richler, Elizabeth Mitchell, Gemma Wain, and Maria Golikova.

© P.

ANDRÉE A. MICHAUD is one of the most beloved and celebrated writers of the Francophonie. She is, among numerous accolades, a two-time winner of the Governor General's Literary Award and has won the Arthur Ellis Award for Excellence in Canadian Crime Writing, the Prix Ringuet, and France's Prix SNCF du Polar. Her novel *Boundary* was longlisted for the Scotiabank Giller Prize and has been published in seven territories. *Back Roads* is Michaud's eleventh novel and the third to be published in English. She was born in Saint-Sébastien-de-Frontenac and continues to live in the province of Quebec.

J. C. SUTCLIFFE is a translator, writer, and editor. She has written for the *Globe and Mail*, the *Times Literary Supplement*, and the *National Post*, among other publications. Her translations include *Mama's Boy* and *Mama's Boy Behind Bars* by David Goudreault, *Document 1* by François Blais, and *Worst Case, We Get Married* by Sophie Bienvenu. *Back Roads* is her first translation for Arachnide.